breach

Olumide Popoola is a Nigerian German writer of long and short fiction, based in London. Her publications include essays, poetry, short stories, the novella *this is not about sadness* and the play text *Also by Mail*. She lectures in creative writing, currently as associate lecturer at Goldsmiths, University of London.

www.olumidepopoola.com

Born in Zambia and raised in Zimbabwe, Annie Holmes left southern Africa and filmmaking to enrol in a writing programme in California. Her short fiction has been published in Zimbabwe and the United States, and she has co-edited two collections of oral narratives in McSweeney's Voice of Witness series: *Hope Deferred* and *Underground America*. She lives in the UK.

Twitter @AnnieHolmesLit

MEIKE ZIERVOGEL
PEIRENE PRESS

I commissioned Olumide Popoola and Annie Holmes to go to the Calais refugee camps to distil stories into a work of fiction about escape, hope and aspiration. On another level, however, these stories also take seriously the fears of people who want to close their borders. It's that dialogue that isn't happening in real life. A work of art can help to bridge the gap.

First published in Great Britain in 2016 by
Peirene Press Ltd
17 Cheverton Road
London N19 3BB
www.peirenepress.com

Designed by Sacha Davison Lunt
Photographic image by Jim Simpson CC by 2.0
Typeset by Tetragon, London
Printed and bound by T J International, Padstow, Cornwall

Peirene

OLUMIDE POPOOLA
AND
ANNIE HOLMES

breach

*For Mohamed K., Diar R.,
and all the others who so
generously told us their stories.*

Counting Down

GPS tells me it's eleven minutes. I don't think that's right. It's too short. How can you cross a border, go from one country to another, and be there in eleven minutes? It took us two weeks to get here.

The others laugh because I say I want them to call me Obama. We are sitting down by a tree to plan the eleven minutes.

'Why not Clinton?' Calculate says. 'At least it would sound like you got some action.'

I don't know what he means; I know some boys who are called Clinton, back at home, in Sudan. It's nothing special. But Calculate is old. I normally wait for him to speak.

It's getting darker, the trees are dipping themselves in silence. The others are looking at their phones. We need to agree on when to start the eleven minutes. We need to plan the forty-nine minutes after that, because if we have to walk all the way to the train station it will be that long.

I don't want to sleep in this country. Not tonight.

I search the others' faces. Why is everyone quiet now? I just want to think big; you have to set your bar high. It's one of the things Calculate has taught me, an expression.

I say to them, 'It's just a little fun. Why not?'

I am disturbing their thoughts. They are busy with more important things. Already these thoughts are like swimming with wet clothes. It's heavy, too much to hold on to. It pulls you back. You could drown.

I have made a habit with this thing, the names and the stories, always distracting them. I think they think that I cannot be quiet. Not when it is needed. Like now. When we are planning the next step, like Calculate says.

Suleyman is coughing. He leans forward; his small chest comes out and he does harh-harh-harh, his tongue tired in his mouth. Earlier today there was a bit of blood in his spit. I check that he is not spitting now. He is leaning back against the tree, pointing his thumb upwards, his eyes closed. He does it all the time, the thumbs up. Even though he himself isn't thumbs up. Not at all. When I first met him his face was round and black. Now he is grey and thin and his eyes are hanging like a bag of shopping.

MG says, 'Or Michelle.'

I throw him a look that tells him to shut his mouth. With my mouth I say, 'You're not funny.'

'You don't understand. You can use it as Michel. It's French. Man's name. I learned in school. Michelle better than Obama. Better brain, my brother says. Nicer to the people, she is really for the people.'

'And beautiful,' Calculate says. He laughs again. 'It would suit you.'

I ignore him and turn my head to the side. He is still wearing the Leicester Hockey Club shirt someone gave him in Puglia. And the fake leather jacket. I told him it wasn't real leather but he said he didn't care. His hair and the jacket match. I think he feels older with it, grown up. MG doesn't usually talk rubbish. His mouth is too quick but he is on his way to being smart. Calculate said it.

I call him MG because he doesn't use Western Union. Only MoneyGram. He thinks it is better. The rates, the service, the staff.

I said to him, 'Hey, little brother, it's just ordinary people. Look at the shops, they are the same: news-agents, small grocers, phone repair shops. Nothing special, same kind, makes no difference if Western Union or MoneyGram.'

The others agreed, but he is not convinced. He taps on his forehead with one finger. It's shiny. It was the same when I first met him. It was hot there, it is not hot now. Still, his face is sweaty. This boy has a tap inside his forehead. It's broken. It drips slowly, always leaving something on his skin. He knocks on that forehead, looking at us, when he wants us to listen. His finger is faster than the dripping of his broken tap that makes all the sweat. He looks ridiculous with his one finger hammering at where his brain is supposed to be. He says he knows, his brother told him. The brother said that they are trying to catch people using Western Union, the smugglers. It is better to leave it alone.

MG put away whatever his brother sent him. Everyone did it that way. Someone sends it, you pick it up later, when you have arrived on safe ground. You couldn't take money in the boat in case you lost it.

But that guy and his brother. I want to push MG sometimes. Push him into the road, just to wake him up. If your brother is so great, why does he not come for you? Why does he not tell you how to get to the UK? To London even. Why does he keep saying, 'I don't know, I don't know, all has changed,' when you call?

'Papers,' MG says, 'no papers.'

'Can you be quiet now? I don't want to get caught here.'

Calculate thinks he is our leader. Because he is older, because MG looks at him – his eyes asking, Is this right? – when we have to make a decision.

I answer that I don't need to be quiet. There is no one here. No one can see us. But Calculate puts his finger on his thin lips and puts his backside on a bit of cardboard he keeps in his bag and leans against the tree that is near Suleyman. He tells me to be quiet again. MG is throwing his eyes at me, shy. I haven't replied to his Michel idea. Why? It's stupid.

GPS moves his shoulders up, then lets them fall. He wants to say sorry that way. Sorry, but Calculate knows what we need to do. I don't understand GPS sometimes. Have we not made it most of the way without Calculate? But I just open my backpack as if I am looking for something, my lips holding each other tight.

When I met MG some days ago I looked at him and said to myself, This guy is scared. Sweating too much. It's just a line, I wanted to say, for you to wait in. Nothing can happen now, little brother. You survived the boat, you have been picked up by the coastguard. You survived the crazy people who want to keep their beach clean, free of refugees. They think refugees make their summer income leave through the back door. Tourism does not want to see any dead bodies floating onto the sand. A man told me this. That man spat in front of my feet. I didn't understand him. That is how I met Calculate. He translated it with his funny Arabic. I didn't spit back. I just nodded. And smiled.

I would never talk to strangers like that in my country. My first lesson in this Europe. But there are others who have a different view. Tourism or not, there is war. People are fleeing. They feel it is their duty. One of those gave me a backpack. She was waiting at the street that runs by the beach. She said there were clean clothes inside. And some food. There was also a note, a postcard written by a child. It said, *Welcome*. And,

We hope that you will be happy and that you will be with family and friends. Safe.

I wanted to say to the sweating boy we didn't yet know, Nothing can happen now. You are in Europe. This was before the man with his opinions and Calculate's translation.

GPS and I smiled at MG. GPS stretched out his hand. The fingers danced in front of his body: it's beautiful. He stopped when they had touched enough air, waited for MG to shake it.

'Welcome to Italy,' he laughed.

MG, who we didn't call MG then, laughed too. His hand went swimming in GPS's. He wiped his face with his T-shirt.

'My brother...'

It was the first thing he said.

GPS says MG is in love with his brother. I think he is just too young. He says he is nineteen but I don't think so. There is no hair on his face.

I said, 'Your brother?'

But he replied, 'Welcome you too.' Then he smiled. Big smile. This is the best thing about MG. Besides the brother who sends money. He can make his face become a curtain that opens fast. He can make it very large, big, happy. First there is nothing, just a boy who pretends to be a man, with a few lines on his face that make him look like an old man Photoshopped onto a baby's picture. Then, sunrise, the movie is starting, the face is already the happy ending. That is how MG smiles.

GPS turned to me.

'I think this is what they mean by cute,' he said.

I agreed.

He asked MG, 'Are you here with your brother?'

'No,' MG replied. 'Alone.'

I didn't ask him, that first day we met, why he was alone. He is too young. Even a mother from his culture would not agree that you can leave your home alone if you are a baby like MG. Even if there is war. But I didn't ask. You can't ask everything. Instead I said, 'They gave us a tent. We need someone to share it with. It's for four people.'

The nights that we have been travelling MG sleeps early – it must be because he is still growing. GPS and I sit together and talk about the future. When we get there. Calculate doesn't sleep until late. He always calls his family, who are still at home, in Syria. He walks off with his short legs, his belly showing under his shirt, phone in hand, his hand scratching his growing beard. I say to GPS that you can still shave, that Calculate could have asked the volunteers for razors. GPS's reply is quick: 'It's not important. That man has other problems, much bigger than shaving.' I think that it is not good to come with a beard that is not even stylish, looking like you have not washed properly. I too have bigger problems than that. Still. But it is me who started, so I leave it.

When he finishes on the phone Calculate wants to talk, always. His shoulders will be hugging his belly, his face so tired he will have to hold it sometimes, his arms on his knee. He will sit next to MG and put his arm around him and MG will put his head on Calculate's shoulder. They will sit like that while Calculate gives us lessons in good English.

I thought MG was calling him uncle, but GPS says it's *baba*. Father.

Calculate says when we arrive we should present ourselves at the first police station. There we claim asylum. I ask him how it works, claiming asylum. He says you just say you are a refugee from Sudan. You want to claim asylum. They will interview us and that is how it starts.

Calculate knows good English because he has studied it. He likes English literature, he says. If he hadn't become an engineer he would have become an English professor. I also studied engineering, so I look at him thinking why. English is good to speak, but it is not a profession. My eyes are wider than they should be, my question is there, anyone can read it. But with my mouth I say, 'I understand.'

Calculate says that what he's teaching us is just some tips, some things his friends who are already in the UK have told him.

'Most people don't know enough,' Calculate says.

MG jumps in. 'Some of us want to go to Germany, some to the UK, others to Denmark, because we don't really know where it is best, who will welcome us.'

That is when Calculate says, 'You are getting very smart.'

MG pulls open the curtain from his face, like he is running out of time. In one second his face is beaming.

There are five trees here. Suleyman is leaning against one, one hand on the grass, the other on his chest. Alghali is sitting next to him and gives him water once in a while, when the harh-harh-harh starts again. Not like laughing but like spitting air out with great force. You can hear the scratching inside his chest. Alghali is so light that I say to him he is just like an Egyptian. He doesn't think it's funny but that is not new to me – he never laughs at my jokes. I think he is worried. How will you present yourself at the police station and say you are from Darfur when your skin looks like you are Arab? But it's not my problem. Alghali is never smiling, his forehead is always making lines, thinking. All of us are thinking a lot, but Alghali makes the most lines on his face.

Suleyman and Alghali cannot be without one another. Like GPS and I, they are good friends. But they never separate, not even to speak to someone.

Ibrahim is sitting by the tree closest to them. He keeps his eyes shut, but I can see he is watching them, trying to be part of whatever they do, as usual. That's why I call them twins plus one. Unnamed. But I never say the unnamed part, it's too long. Sometimes I say to them that they are only six days old. It's a joke, because in my country you get your name seven days after you're born. The whole village comes and looks at you. Although you are covered up because of the evil eye, still the whole village will come to greet you and to hear your name. If you don't have a name you must be less than seven days old. The twins plus one don't laugh. Their eyes are tired. I talk too much.

Ibrahim takes out some water and offers it to Suleyman. It's stupid. Alghali is already doing that. But he wants to be more than plus one – he wants to belong to them. Good luck with that.

Calculate's phone is ringing. He gets up to walk down the hill for privacy.

We met Calculate in Puglia. All of a sudden there was this man by our side, pretending to be our friend, walking with us. I didn't notice the three standing by a street corner. *Bang!* I walked straight into Alghali, our heads knocking together. They were about to get upset because they thought I wanted to make them angry. Calculate looked behind him. He was coming from the police station, but no one had followed him. So he explained how it was all his fault, my walking into the twins plus one. We started talking.

Here we are now, making plans for eleven and forty-nine minutes.

'Distant relations, you are,' Calculate says, because GPS and Alghali are third cousins. But because they have never met before they only move their shoulders up and down, quickly so Calculate does not really notice. Calculate sums it up: 'It's not very close.' He explains that 'sum' is used in different ways but that summing up is also something that we might have to do in the future. When it comes. The summing up of our situation. Of what is going on in our country.

'When you claim asylum you sum it all up.' He laughs and his eyes become so small they fade into his unshaven face until you only see two lines with a little hair.

I can make jokes at any time but even I don't understand why he laughs. 'How do you sum up genocide?'

He is quiet after that.

I tell GPS that I think Calculate likes to be a philosopher, but GPS says it is just because Calculate wanted to be an English professor and now he has to compensate for it. Both of his hands are open like a question. The long fingers curled upwards, his shoulders raised. I know he learned it from Calculate. To compensate for something. I heard them, but I was busy thinking of a new name.

MG is taking out his sleeping bag and lying on top of it. He looks at me.

I say, 'Lots of time.'

He closes his eyes.

*

The first night the twins plus one and Calculate stayed with us, Calculate said I should come and walk with him.

He asked, 'That boy, MG, where are his people?'

I shook my head. 'I don't know. I met him yesterday, changing money.'

'He's alone?'

'I think so.'

Calculate didn't have the beard yet, but he was already scratching it. We walked for a bit longer, then he showed me.

'I have been here for two weeks. See over there?'

We had reached another campsite. It was a stupid question. Why not just say what you have to say? But of course I didn't know Calculate then, so I just made 'Mmh' with my mouth.

'I was staying there. I met some kids. They were by themselves. I shared my food with them every day. One of them was waiting for his uncle. They had been separated on the journey, but now the uncle had found out where his nephew was staying and was on his way. One morning the children were gone. Disappeared. Except for one of the bigger boys. Men had come and forced his friends inside a van. He ran and hid. Two days later the uncle arrived. No one had heard from his nephew.'

Calculate stood there for a long time. He didn't say anything else. After a while he wiped his forehead.

'Let's go.'

Before we got back to the others he said we must take care of MG. All of us. He didn't want the same to happen to him. I said, 'That's why I said stay with us. He's too young. You cannot make it alone.'

That first night Calculate slept with us in the tent. Next to MG. They whispered in their funny Arabic I couldn't understand until it was only Calculate's voice and MG's breathing.

Calculate is coming back.

No one has said whether they will call me Obama.

Calculate says, 'It's almost time. Make sure you are ready. We can't wait until it's completely dark.'

What we need to get ready for I don't know. We are ready. We were just waiting so it's dark enough for us not to be seen. MG has his eyes closed again but he can jump from deep sleep to 100-metre race. I saw it when we left our tent in Puglia. And GPS is just staring into the space that is getting blue and grey, the shadows dropping behind the trees. His eyes are far away. GPS loves being quiet. Like MG's curtain opens when he smiles, GPS's face closes. He needs to lock it so nothing can come in and nothing can leave. Then it's just him. No one else.

When it's me and him I can make him laugh. He will say, 'You're not as funny as you think,' but he will still laugh.

Like when I told him, 'I know now! Twins plus one.'

And he looked at me with his *what now?* look. I pointed at Ibrahim, Suleyman and Alghali.

He laughed.

I put my hand on GPS's shoulder. He jumps a little. He hasn't yet come back from where he went this time.

'We're getting ready.'

I don't believe it will take eleven minutes. Everything so far has taken longer.

It's quiet. Nobody is saying anything. I can only see where my feet are touching the street and the edge of a field on this side. The houses have stopped. Calculate and MG are ahead of us – I saw their shadows passing the sign. I check my phone. They made it in nine minutes. Calculate wanted to see whether all was clear. If not he would warn us, because Suleyman cannot run today. They will be waiting for us. I wasn't in the mood to hurry myself. Why? Eleven is eleven. It's not less than eleven.

The twins plus one, GPS and I are walking by the side of the street. We make it in seventeen minutes. That's good enough.

There is nothing special on the other side. It looks the same. But now we are in France.

I can hear his ringtone, an old pop song, before I can see his shadow. I have heard it so many times in the last few days it drives me crazy. I said to GPS, 'Why can't he put it on vibrate?' I don't want someone to notice us. GPS agreed. We arrive where they are waiting for us. Calculate answers his phone and walks off.

He is back in less than two minutes, sweating.

'Let's go.'

It is annoying. We were going. We only stopped because of him. But I cannot say this. I look at GPS; my eyes are rolling, but he doesn't see it. Calculate rushes ahead now, pulling MG with him. He walks arm in arm, but I can see it's not to be close to MG. Not this time. It's because he wants to show us that we are too slow for him. MG turns around, confused, but there is nothing he likes more than being close to Calculate. Except talking about his brother.

Ibrahim says, 'We can't walk all the way to the train station. We have to stop somewhere to rest. Suleyman –'

But Calculate has already gone. I don't think he knows where he's going. GPS hasn't even shown him the map on the phone. But this is the only street here. After some time, we see them waiting.

'We better –' Ibrahim is pointing with his head at Suleyman. He is really trying today, trying to become three instead of plus one.

MG and Calculate are like stones. The air has run away from them. Calculate has one knee on the ground, MG's black plastic bag and his leather jacket in front of him.

'I was only checking.'

MG's face, which can shine like the sun, is closed. Much more than GPS's has ever been. His body is shaking as if he is on vibrate and someone is calling him on repeat. I walk up to him.

'What's wrong, little brother?'

'I went for a pee over there…' MG's voice is crawling over his lips.

GPS asks Calculate, 'What happened?'

'Nothing.'

Calculate gets up. There is money in his hand.

'I was just checking to see what is left –'

'It's not yours! It's mine! My brother sent it.'

'I was just trying… We are all tired, we need to take the train.'

MG presses his eyes shut.

Calculate is getting angry now.

'I need to get to Calais. I have to make the last train. Someone is waiting for me.'

I still try to understand what I am seeing. Since we first met, Calculate has called MG 'son'.

'An agent. It's already paid… My family, they are waiting. Waiting for me to get them out.'

Calculate is angry because all his things were stolen in Puglia. He has nothing but his good English. He went to the police. I wanted to ask him if he was stupid but now that I know him I think that his anger makes him do things no one can understand. Not even he himself. He didn't think. Next thing he was standing in a police station and someone wanted to fingerprint him. But you can't get fingerprinted there. Unless you want to stay. Italy is like Greece. Collapsed. There is no future there. It won't come if you stay. Your future will disappear. And I have already seen that. In my own village.

That's when he ran, found us, walked off with us as if we were friends.

I step forward and take the money out of Calculate's hand. It's more than twenty euros. Enough for the train but not enough for two. MG takes the money, tears on his face. GPS comes over too and touches his hair.

Calculate is standing with his hands open, like GPS did when he told me about *to compensate*. His shoulders are trying to say sorry, they sweep the floor. But his mouth does other things.

'I have a son. A *real* son. I left him. They are waiting for me... I need to...'

Alghali says, 'We have shared whatever we have with each other. Not by force, not by theft, but by choice.'

Suleyman speaks too: it sounds like it hurts him. 'Just because we put it all together doesn't mean you can take it.'

But Calculate's cleverness has collapsed – he is losing everything he knows.

'Do you understand? There is a boy like you waiting for me to get him to safety. My son, my real son.'

MG pushes us away. He looks at Calculate. Nobody is making a sound. He takes some time, then he clears his throat. His lips form an O; his tongue helps to push it out, the spit. It lands, summing everything up, right in front of Calculate.

We all move now. All of us. Except Calculate. I say to MG, 'Adnan, you really are someone.'

MG smiles. It's sad but he is also proud. I have never called him by his name.

'I have it from my brother.'

We walk for a bit without talking. Calculate is behind but he is too far gone – he is not part of the group any more.

MG says, 'Thank you,' turning to all of us.

I ask, 'For what?'

He puts his arm through mine and through GPS's on the other side and starts walking again.

'Welcome to France, Michelle.'

Suleyman starts laughing, but his chest pushes up too much and he holds it, bending over, coughing. Harh-harh-harh. GPS opens his face; the laughter falls out like his hands: beautiful and long.

The Terrier

My concern on that particular afternoon was to prevent the boy from walking into the bathroom, where Luc was on his knees, swearing. I call Luc a friend. We've known each other for many years, so I'm aware of his politics. Now, I don't lie, not for anyone, certainly not to placate Luc, but it would be so much easier if the boy – I could hear him walking up the path – did not appear at the bathroom door. He wouldn't need to say a single one of his new French words. Luc is no fool and his brother lives close to that open space on the dunes near the harbour where the camp is, the place they're calling the Jungle, so Luc is familiar with the migrants who stay there. He would recognise the young man's olive skin, his dark eyes, in an instant. His stance, even, would give him away. And what do I know? A plumber like Luc, so attuned to the stink of shit, might pick up some odour from the life in that dirty camp.

But he didn't appear, the boy, thank God. I heard him start across the kitchen, then turn back to remove his shoes and leave them by the door, as I'd asked him to. Why he goes back to that camp, day after day, in the wind and cold and rain, now that they have rooms in this warm house, I don't know, but I'm not having him tramp filth and disease into my establishment. Next, he padded down the passage in his socks to his sister's room, knocked on the door and went in. Sometimes they shout at each other in there, or she wails and cries, but that day, the day she blocked the toilet, they only murmured and I was relieved.

Luc heard them and looked up at me, plunger in one plastic-gloved hand, his lips turned down like a cartoon character. 'Foreign?' he asked and I nodded. Luc snorted. He thinks I'm crazy, allowing strangers into my home. If he'd known these two were not tourists but refugees, dear God, I hate to think what he'd have said. He loses no chance to rail against them, all of them, with their tents and shacks. Trash strewn far and wide, and the noise at night, terrible thumping music distorted on the wind, waking his brother in his own bed. How are his nieces to walk safely with all those men hanging around? Luc holds the bald bowl of his head in his hands when he starts to rage. It burns him. He could spit. Sometimes he does, but not in my bathroom.

Let me be frank, I wouldn't miss Luc as a friend, but a good plumber is hard to replace.

I walked him to his van when he was done, the bloody cotton wool extracted and the flush functional again. But I'd caught Luc's anger, or perhaps it was the strain of keeping those two a secret. I closed the kitchen door hard, stamped through the house and knocked on the girl's door. My home, for God's sake. My grandparents' farmhouse. I might welcome the city council's money in these lean winter months – especially since tourists were being scared off by news footage of rampaging migrants on the motorway – but by God I wouldn't have this disrespect for my property.

Bang, bang, bang.

The boy opened the door. On the bed behind him, his sister hugged her knees and bent her head, her face hidden by the headscarf.

'She is sorry, madame,' he said. 'She apologises. I apologise for her.'

He didn't look contrite. What I felt from him was defeat but with something iron hard beneath it. A proud rage.

I couldn't let it go.

'It's no good,' I said. Seeing them there, my anger was fading, but I blew on the ashes. I spoke firmly. 'You need to take more care,' I said.

He bowed his head. Then he drew a few notes from the pocket of his jeans, euros, grubby and worn, and made to offer them to me.

'Don't be ridiculous,' I said.

It was the worst thing to say. His eyes turned icy. The girl sniffed back tears, looking up at me from the bed.

It's you who are ridiculous, I told myself. I put my hand on his arm. 'No, no,' I said. 'The insurance will

29

pay for the toilet. But your sister needs pads and there's a bin in the bathroom –'

But he cut me off. It horrified him. 'I cannot talk about these things, madame,' he said.

He almost pushed me aside in his haste to leave. The girl watched him go, then put her head down and cried some more. The kitchen door slammed and I heard his quick footsteps on the gravel. Heading back to the camp, I supposed, even though it was getting dark. It called him, that place. People there spoke his language, something shared. Whereas my home, my home tongue, everything French, he wanted to escape.

The girl sat folded over herself on the child's bed. My old bed, in fact, in the room where I used to sleep when I visited Grand-mère and Grand-père, and still my favourite room in the house, decorated now with a nautical theme for smaller visitors – floorboards painted white, seashells on the windowsills and a crisp blue-and-white-striped duvet. Shipshape. And here, under the bright stripes, this forlorn stranger. Her time of the month and I'd made no provision for it. It hadn't crossed my mind.

I dug around in my drawer of guest toiletries to find the pads that I'd bought when I'd first inherited the farm and started the bed and breakfast. I drew the girl by the hand to the bathroom to show her the roll of plastic bags in a drawer and the little bin. I pointed through the window at the big bin outside where she could throw the bags away. It was all done in sign language and my basic English – she had no word of French and barely any English either – and she nodded quietly at each instruction. Unlike her brother's, her eyes are eerily blue, blue-green but transparent in the way that clear water flowing over sand is transparent, full of light. She generally kept them downcast or fixed on her brother, so it was arresting, it gave me pause, to have her meet my eyes so directly.

I called her into the kitchen and put the kettle on to make tea. She surprised me then, coming over to where I stood and putting her hands on my waist, looking up at me from under her headscarf – I'm not tall but she is tiny – and then burying her face in my neck, planting three breathy kisses there. Like butterfly wings beating, I thought, and I am not a woman who is given to fanciful notions.

I call him Omid, the young man. It's the name he asked me to use when they arrived, he and his sister, and he said I was to call the girl Nalin. They'd stood on the doorstep at first, behind the official from the city council, in the kind of bulky jackets you'd wear for camping or farming, her headscarf under the green jacket hood. The first thing I noticed about him was how tired he seemed: not physically, not in the sense that he needed sleep, although perhaps that too, but a weariness in his eyes and his voice. Old before his time, as the saying goes.

'Who is this in the photograph?' he asked me in the dining room the morning after Luc's visit. I was toasting bread for their morning meal. Not my home-baked bread, I should say, which I make with coarse-ground wholewheat and a seed-rich crust, but rather a sliced brown loaf from Lidl. They wouldn't know the difference, I told myself. They're not about to rate my cooking on TripAdvisor.

I assumed he meant the photograph of my grandfather, family hero, wartime Resistance fighter. Everyone asks about Grand-père. But when I turned, it was a different photograph he was looking at.

'That's me,' I said. 'And that's the same motorbike that's out there on the path, under the cover.'

He walked past the shrouded bike every day on his way to or from the camp, but now he looked out of the window to check, then back at the photograph.

'This is you, madame?'

In the photo, I am wearing tight jeans, an air of bravado and no helmet. Today, I'm a little stouter perhaps, and my hair is short, but otherwise not so different, I wouldn't have thought.

'You ride that big bike, madame?'

I would've liked to claim that I rode it every day, just to shock him, but, as I have said, lying is not something that I do easily.

'Hardly ever,' I said.

'Ha!' he said. 'I want to see that, madame. I want to see you ride that bike.'

I hadn't seen him smile before, not in this open way, almost grinning. Before this, when he had smiled it had been from politeness, a wan expression wrung out of grim depths. Now I could see the boy he was meant to be, amused and handsome.

Nalin asked him something in Kurdish and he replied and she got up from the breakfast table to peer at the photograph with him and smile at me and giggle. Who had they thought me before this? An ageless crone, without any life or history of my own? And why not, really? Why should they have any attention to spare from their own predicament? When I brought fresh toast from the kitchen, I patted the top of Nalin's head as I went back to boil the kettle.

I had no idea how long they would stay, these two. When the city official brought them that first day, she didn't tell me and I didn't ask. She was concerned with the here and now: how the council would transfer payment to my account, what costs I could and could not expect to be refunded. In the newspapers and on television, the press goaded the government from every side, some demanding, as Luc did, that they close the camp and send these people away, and others, outraged, attacking the authorities for abandoning refugee children in that camp in winter. I'd accepted payment in advance for both my rooms for two weeks, including all meals. I was living in the present too, of course: how to cover my heating bill after almost a month with no guests. A few days later, I called the office. The man asked for the refugees' names. I told him the names they'd given me, but they rang no bells so I gave my name instead. Well, the official said, he could see the record but unfortunately no, he couldn't tell me when the council would move them. He would ask. He would call me back.

As if bureaucrats call anyone back. It wasn't like I was turning away reservations, so I let it rest. I told none of my acquaintances that they were here, this sister and brother, in my house – no one from my bridge club, not even Marianne when we spoke, as usual, a few times every week. At first I was embarrassed, perhaps even ashamed, to be earning money in this way. But it's my own business and nobody else's, I told myself. It's not as though I'm lying to anyone.

Next day, when I drove in at the gate, Omid ran out to help me bring in the shopping, pulling up the hood of his jacket against the drizzle, splashing through the puddles in the driveway. It surprised me to find Nalin standing in her coat by the kitchen door. She held the door open for me and Omid.

'Nalin is lonely,' Omid said. 'We go to see her friend.'

She questioned him in Kurdish – asking what he'd said, I guessed – and he replied, an impatient big-brother tone in his voice. On the kitchen table, I saw a note. 'We go to see our friends,' it said. So they had meant to be gone before I returned. This I approved of. It pleased me, somehow, that they asked me so little. If I wanted to help them, it was purely my own decision. I too am proud. I don't like to be pushed.

'I must go into town now,' I told them. 'I will give you a ride to the camp.'

'Oh no, madame,' Omid said. 'I know a short way to walk there.'

'But your sister will get wet.'

And so they climbed in, Nalin in the back, Omid beside me in the passenger seat. They were quiet; we didn't speak. In the rear-view mirror, I could see Nalin looking out of the window and I realised that she hadn't left the house since she first entered it more than a week before. I'd served their food and left them to it, just as I would have with any of my guests. Oh, that's not true. With most guests I would also talk a little, and then a little more if they had questions. That's what people want in a B&B: good food, some charm, a few local stories but not too much. I am the host and cook, not a friend.

The camp is not very far from my grandparents' small farm, but I seldom use that last stretch of the motorway. It leads only to the harbour, the ferries and a flat stretch of small factories – I have little call to go that way in general and no inclination since the tents began to appear on the sand. I see the camp on the news and the internet and that's enough. To be frank, I felt some anxiety about driving that way. How abruptly we swept off the motorway and down towards the blue tents. A few police officers stood by a white police van at the bottom of the slope and I saw that the camp began right there, almost underneath the motorway. The tarmac road turned sharply to the left and away, while the dirt track to the right led into the mass of tents and shacks.

There were people everywhere, some walking under the motorway, beside the high concrete graffiti-covered walls and out the other side, ignoring the police, ignoring my little car as I pulled over.

'Thank you, madame,' Omid said as he opened the door.

Directly ahead of the car was a simple wooden shed of pale new planks, a storefront faced with chicken wire, a man behind the counter. Beside the shop, on the low swell of a dune, was a tent, no more than a pup tent but with two sections, one of them open, and a pair of brown shoes visible there, side by side. Someone's home. I imagined crawling in, leaving my sandy shoes just inside, out of the rain, crawling through to sleep in there.

Too late, I thought of giving Nalin my umbrella. They were gone, walking fast along the dirt track, not looking back. I leaned over to open the passenger door and close it properly. As I locked it, the man behind the plank counter gave me a mild wave of greeting. Like any shopkeeper in any village anywhere. That surprised me more than anything. People passed behind and in front of the car, so I had to wait before I could reverse out safely. A policewoman cradling a rifle ducked her head to look in at me as I drove by, but without much interest. All along the road, drab factories on one side faced the new white fence along the other side, hemming the train tracks and topped with scrolls of white barbed wire. Despite the rain, men paced along the fence, alone or in groups, not hurrying, not like they had places to go but rather time to kill.

Even though I had stayed in the car, barely opening the door at the camp entrance, I felt that I must wash my hands when I got home. I felt gritty, as though I had in fact crawled into that pup tent. This is what comes of going too close, I told myself. You lose all perspective. I kept myself busy with laundry and then I picked fruit in the orchard, but my mind was on the world, the under-world, that I'd glimpsed from its edge, the figures pacing the high white fence along the railway line, shoulders up against the cold, hands deep in coat pockets, dark heads bent. Like figures from history or documentaries, I realised, like second-hand memories of war.

'It doesn't look like a jungle, that camp,' I said to Omid when he came home, after dark, his coat wet.

'What does a jungle look like, madame?'

'Thick with trees and creepers and bushes, with birds and animals.'

'A jungle,' he said, 'is a place for animals only. And that is a jungle, I tell you, madame.'

'Get dry,' I told him. 'I will make tea.'

Nalin had stayed there, in the camp. In the cold. She would sleep with another family in their shelter.

'I made that shelter,' Omid told me, sitting at the table in the kitchen. 'With some volunteers. Of all the Kurdish families, I am the one to speak English. Or,' he corrected himself, 'the good English. They need me there.'

'And why does Nalin want to stay there?'

'She miss her friend,' he said. 'There is another girl there, younger, twelve years old. They talk. She is safe with that family.'

'But the cold?'

'She sleep with the mother and the daughters. They make warm together,' he said. I set a cup of tea in front of him and he looked down at it. 'But also,' he said, 'water falls.' He mimed drops from above.

'The roof leaks?'

'No, no, no.' He was affronted again. 'The shelter is strong. But at night…'

'Condensation?' I said, and he nodded.

I meant to leave it there – I wasn't going to get too close – but I heard myself say that he seemed worried.

'In the jungle, good and bad people. All mix,' he said. 'Before we come here, I keep her in the shelter. And always I stay nearby. Men, too many men…' He shook his head. 'Some women, they have no money to pay smuggler.'

'Did you pay smuggler?' My English, never fluent, became even more abrupt and approximate, echoing his.

'Of course I pay.'

I sat down across the table from him, kept my eyes on him. He shrugged and, in his exhausted flat voice, told me about the money. After his father was killed and they'd left Syria, he and his sister, he'd saved some money, working in Turkey in a car wash and as a waiter in a restaurant. Nalin had sold her gold. He'd paid 900 euros for two places on a boat across to Greece (vomiting on board, wading drenched to the shore, a fire on the beach, kind Greek fishermen bringing food). From Greece to Macedonia, forty euros for tickets for a bus, seven hours.

'Wait, wait,' I said. I brought my laptop to the table to follow the journey on Google Maps.

'In Macedonia, they give us a piece of paper to get to Serbia by train. Now, we have no money. We sleep two nights in a bus station. From Serbia to Croatia, then to Hungary we go by train, 4,000 people in one train, free for everyone. Hungary to Austria.'

I tracked the story with my finger across the map on the screen, zooming in, zooming out. It was a saga he was describing, an odyssey. No – I recalled the mass of figures I'd seen on the news, trudging across Eastern Europe – it was something more brutal, like a forced march. I glanced up at the portrait of Grand-père, Resistance hero. It crossed my reluctant mind that he'd have taken a stand if he were still alive. He'd have been on the side of the weary marchers.

'In Germany, in Passau city,' Omid continued, 'the police catch us in the train station. They want to take my fingerprints. I say, "I don't want to stay in this country because I have family in UK." They say, "No problem, it's just for numbers." I say, "I don't want, I don't want," but they force us.'

As he recounted this, he clenched his fists, tucking in his thumb, hiding his prints.

'Why didn't you want to give your fingerprints?'

'It is law in Europe. Where they take your prints, that is the country you must get asylum. I must not get stuck, madame. I must find my mother.'

He uncurled his fingers and we both looked down at his palms, open on the kitchen table. His future, quite literally, in his hands, at his fingertips. Then he smiled up at me, his old man's tired, ironic smile on his boy's face.

I wanted to give him something, so I stepped out onto the terrace to collect the quinces I had picked. The strong scent of the fruit filled the dining room and Omid let his head fall back. 'Perfume,' he said. He closed his eyes and breathed it.

He hated to ask for anything, that boy. It offended him, his honour. But the laptop stood open on the table next to the fruit basket and now he asked if he could use it to check his emails.

I don't offer it to guests – they can use the Wi-Fi on their own devices – but this boy could barely hold on to his boots, his sister or his fingerprints on that journey, never mind a computer.

'Not every day,' I said, 'but now, today, you may.'

I looked over his shoulder as he typed in his address on Gmail. It ended with what looked like a date.

'Ah,' I said, making conversation. 'Year of your birth – 1994?'

He looked alarmed. 'No,' he said. 'Not 1994, 1999. I am a minor. I am seventeen.'

The quince-scented moment had passed. Omid banged hard on the keys, typing in a foreign language, hurrying to be done and gone. I gritted my teeth to stop myself telling him not to pound, to type softly. This is why I must keep my life and my things to myself, my thoughts went. It was only after he'd closed Gmail and given a curt thank you on his way to his room that I came to wonder about the question of age. He didn't look seventeen years old to me. Why lie to me? What other lies might he be telling? He said Nalin was fourteen but she might be older too. Perhaps she wasn't even his sister. Perhaps they weren't refugees at all, but criminals, or even terrorists.

My dreams were turbulent that night, but not seething with anxiety about the lies that Omid might be telling. Instead, his story of crossing the sea to Greece set me on a boat all night, through the dark. It wasn't a dream of empathy, however – it concerned myself, as all dreams do, I suppose. As the waves rose and fell, the dream dinghy crashed from zenith to trough and I was thrown out, first high into the air, then down into the surging water. I laboured desperately through the waves to reach the boat; I clawed at the rubber surface seeking purchase; I reached for the rope ringing the boat edge, the lashing; but again and again I slipped back, down into the depths, weaker each time.

Waking at last, exhausted, the winter morning still dark, I was pinned to the mattress by a heavy grey melancholy. I understood that I am now old. Whatever new waves rise beneath me, I will fail to catch them, to rise in the way I have always risen before. The adventurer on the motorcycle is gone. I am an old woman. The tide subsides.

Nalin came back happier. Girlish. She hugged me in the kitchen. What had she been doing with her friend in the Jungle? 'We sew,' she told me. And when she grew up, what did she want to do then? She gave answers, Omid translated: 'Well, she said she'd like to be a housekeeper, or a fashion designer. Or no! A crime reporter on television.' She ragged her brother (if he was in fact her brother) about his typing skills. He was back on my laptop, pounding away at the keys, and I asked where he'd learned English.

'Facebook,' he said. 'I have many friends in US. And Norway.'

'Pff!' Nalin said. 'He don't know English. Is lazy. He don't study.'

'And you?' I asked her. 'Do you study?'

'She knows nothing,' Omid said. 'I do everything for her.'

But he was smiling. She swatted him with her table napkin.

Perhaps they were lovers, like the fake 'brother and sister' in that Terrence Malick movie, *Days of Heaven*. All this time, everything I knew about them I'd heard from Omid. It was more than the language barrier – he kept Nalin tucked behind him, he spoke for her. But then again, he'd had to protect her across God knows how many thousands of kilometres.

'Madame,' Nalin said, settling down on the chair beside mine at the table, teacup in her hand. 'Kurdish language. I teach you.'

She called out words, I tried to spell them phonetically in roman script and Omid made corrections in capitals, pressing hard on the paper, along with the Kurdish version, each symbol a kind of artwork. 'Hello' and 'How are you?' and 'I am fine'. I could remember only *supas* – 'thank you'. Pronounced, it sounded to me, like *s'pass*.

'How old were you when you left Syria?' I asked, out of the blue. Omid looked up sharply. He translated for Nalin and they consulted in Kurdish.

'I was ten and she was six,' Omid said.

So unconvincing, I found them. How old when they arrived in Turkey? How old when they left Turkey? I was a terrier – I would not let go. Nalin's sweet face fell. Omid turned resentful. I kept asking, interrogating. I couldn't help it. I wanted to understand if they were lying to me, and if so why. Their answers were hesitant and unhappy.

'Thank you for tea, madame,' Omid said, standing when I paused for breath.

'*S'pass*,' I said brightly, but neither of them even smiled. 'If you want to learn French I can teach you,' I said.

Omid turned in the doorway and shook his head. 'English is international language, madame,' he said.

Nalin wouldn't look me in the eye.

They left. Of course. Back to the camp.

Late that afternoon, my friend Marianne called, as she does most days. Conversation is best, I find, when there's no real news, only jokes and memories and random reflections. But Marianne wanted to talk about the refugees and the camp, of all things. What a mess. How would Calais ever get rid of them? She'd seen on Facebook that very day, she said, photographs of a fire in the camp. 'You can't blame Calais locals,' she said. 'It must be very trying. Maybe this is the only way to get rid of them – smoke them out.'

From high on my wall, heroic Grand-père looked down at me from his frame. 'They're human beings, Marianne,' I said. 'And when was this fire?'

'Today! Right now, I tell you.'

I said goodbye and pulled on my coat. The sun was already setting along the low, flat horizon as I drove, one of those absurdly riotous sunsets that my tourists like, crimson streaking into fuchsia. Today, though, it put me in mind of flames. Or blood.

I knew exactly where I'd park – outside one of the factories a few streets away from the camp. My unconscious had perhaps been rehearsing this journey because I did not hesitate. I saw no fire engines, though, no flames, no French vigilantes. I strode up to the storefront, to enquire of the shopkeeper who'd waved at me before.

'Many fires in the jungle,' he said. 'Today, I hear it is a gas bottle exploding.'

I nodded. Beside his shop, the pup tent was zipped up. It was even smaller than I'd remembered.

'Well, I'm here now,' I told the shopkeeper, 'so I might as well go into the camp.' As if he cared. I bought a bottle of water from him. It cost more than at Lidl.

'I am looking for a Kurdish family,' I said, and he directed me towards the area where, he told me, Kurds had their shelters and tents.

'Ask there,' he said.

No one paid me any attention as I walked. Not the volunteers, speaking English, French, Dutch and German. Not the police patrol, like Lego figures in bulletproof black, four and five abreast. And not the refugees, walking in twos and threes up and down the rough tracks. I passed a set of taps on a wooden stand and noticed one man in particular among those gathered there to wash. He'd rolled his trousers up his fat legs and was holding a large naked foot under the cold water. I shivered. Where on earth did Nalin wash here? Where did she go when she had her period?

I caught snatches of language, none familiar to me, bar the volunteers' chatter. I passed many more stores and also structures labelled cafés and I saw the spire of a home-made-looking church behind a wall.

'Kurds?' I asked people. 'Kurds from Syria?' And they pointed me onward: 'Turn right over there.' I passed a marquee where Hare Krishnas seemed to be handing out food. People stood around with bowls, a few women and children along with the men. What would Marianne say, I wondered, if she could see me now, in the almost dark in the refugee camp? Or

Luc the plumber, glowering from his brother's house nearby?

Omid was surprised to see me, when a neighbour showed me to his particular shelter and I knocked on the door. I could see him hesitate. He wanted to send me away, but Nalin came up behind him and drew me into the square box of a room. I left my boots at the door, with other boots, and sat down on the floor. It was like being inside a slow cooker, the sides lined in that silver astronaut paper, like tin foil. Grubby backpacks hung from nails on the walls and more bags were piled in a corner, out of the rain. Sitting cross-legged against the far wall was a bearded Englishman.

'This is Murray,' Omid said.

'I am Eloise,' I told Murray, reaching over our socked feet to shake his hand.

'Eloise,' Nalin repeated. She'd never heard my name before.

'Murray will help us to get to UK,' Omid said. 'To join our mother.'

'Oh, that's good,' I said.

'Because we are minors,' Omid said. 'And minors can perhaps join their family in UK. A new law.'

He must be seventeen, I saw that now. He had to be, or else he would be left here.

I understood him to be floundering in the choppy dark sea of my dream, bearing Nalin along through the waves and then lifting her into the boat, with every chance of being left to sink by himself.

'Oh,' I said again. 'A law for minors.'

'Age,' said Murray. 'It can be a problem when some-one doesn't have a birth certificate. The authorities tend to make arbitrary judgements based only on their impressions.'

Like I had.

'Well,' I said, 'they stay with me, these two, for some time now and I can say for sure that they are minors.'

All three looked at me. I never lie. I hate to lie. But this lying, if it was in fact lying, I was prepared to do. Let's say it was for Grand-père.

But what happened was that Omid held up a folder.

'For us,' he said, 'is not a problem. We have birth certificates.'

'And perhaps,' Nalin said, 'we give our blood.'

'To show it matches our mother's blood,' Omid said.

Nalin held her hand forward, thumb extended towards Murray, like a hitchhiker's. Her thumb for the pricking, for the blood, for the proof. Fingerprints. Age. Genes. DNA. Proofs of the body.

Murray finished making notes in his file and stood to leave, promising to be in touch, to send forms and to arrange for a lawyer in the UK to speak with their mother. I waited by the shelter as Omid and Nalin said goodbye to their friends, and then we three walked back to my car and drove home in the dark. By the back door, I patted the handlebars of my old motorbike. That's another one that'll be moving out of here soon.

Extending a Hand

You sit on the side of the road, Mariam and you. The reception isn't working inside today. Just that annoying crackling you get when someone is on the line, and most of the time there are no bars at all. Outside, here, passing the bridge that hangs over the side of the camp, with the towering fence, it is easier to get a signal. It's also quieter.

The kerb is a little cool but dry. A few people are walking up and down the street that leads straight into the camp. Mainly volunteers, mostly Brits, who park their cars or vans and then move on to the show inside. And it is indeed: the display of poor refugees, the lack of humane conditions. They, the ones who give up their time, are here to extend a helping hand, to help make things survivable. But you don't need a hand; you have two of those. What you need is opportunities.

It is sunny, thank goodness, and warmer than it should be for the time of year. You have clean new clothes on that were given out yesterday. The hoodie is a deep purple, with little yellow triangles on the front and the back. The stretch denims have that washed-out effect you like. It feels good today, with clean clothes, with the sun shining on your face. Mariam is talking about her mother again. You don't want to think about anyone. It is enough to call, briefly, and be called. In between you want to forget that you are here and they are at home, and that *here* is not where you meant to end up at all. You nod along and hear about the ulcer that needs medical attention. Mariam's mother has been asking her to send money for treatment. The local hospital is booked up, she has been waiting for weeks. The private clinic is too expensive. Mariam hasn't told her mother that she isn't anywhere yet. That she is living off donations. You told her from the beginning that that was a mistake: 'Just tell her and then you can talk to each other like mother and daughter.' But Mariam is the optimist of the two of you. She thinks of good outcomes; she leaps ahead. It would be three days, one week at the most here. Why worry her ageing mother with details of a place she wasn't going to stay in long enough to understand its rules?

'You have to tell her. How long will you keep it up? She will be disappointed if you don't send her money.'

'I could make some.'

You look at her and raise your eyebrows. It's easy to make money here, especially for a woman, but there is a price. And it's not the right one. Someone would think he could own you.

The wind is picking up. Mariam huddles against you.

You stand for a second to pull up the tight trousers so they don't expose your backside. There is a gap between your skin and the jeans. You are tiny but your backside can give any of the big girls a run for their money. Mariam says it all the time and laughs. No one makes trousers for your shape. The pair you picked yesterday aren't the loose-fitting ones volunteers think are suitable for this place because you can layer them, as someone said. You gave her the silent treatment when she was trying to make the case, holding up an over-sized pair of second-hand hiking trousers. Why people think they know what's best for you when they are not you, you don't understand. Why you wouldn't know how you want to dress at your age is beyond you. The woman didn't say anything else after that; she turned her face away for the rest of their *one line*, the thing they shout during the distribution of food, clothes, building materials, tents, wood. She stayed, but she didn't have any more advice to offer. You had asked for leggings, tighter jeans, something that would make you feel like you were still twenty-four and not just a refugee squatting in a camp that the locals want gone. Leggings are in fact more comfortable, more practical. You don't have to remember to pull them up when stepping over the endless mud. They won't flap around and you know where they are: close to your body.

When it was your turn and you stood in front of the open van doors, doors that had two volunteers on each side with outstretched arms to help everyone queue, she let you scramble to the cardboard box in the back of the vehicle and choose your own pair. She didn't say anything, just pointed. Dignity involves choosing your own outfits, at least, doesn't it? Doesn't it?

Mariam shuffles to create some heat between you. Her phone is ringing and she waits for it to stop.

'What shall I tell her?'

'The truth. You might need her help. You know that.'

Mariam redials. A van has parked opposite you. It seems that the two women inside have already distributed whatever they had fund-raised for or collected at home. They are in no hurry to get anywhere. They stretch, leaving the front doors open. On a day like this, sunny with its pretence of calm, it's almost like any other short trip but even better: the satisfaction of having done good work, important in fact. Without these people coming and some of them staying, the camp would be nothing like it is. You would suffer a lot more. You know that.

One of the women is changing a little baby on the passenger seat. The second one now looks at you and smiles. You are tired of the visitors who all need acknowledgement, who need you to engage so they can feel that they are doing the right thing. It is not that you don't appreciate their help. What they do keeps you alive. But the rules of it are annoying. You have, in fact, more important things to do. To plan and arrange the next step, if you can even talk about arranging here.

A song pops into your head as the woman moseys towards you. 'Do They Know It's Christmas?'

It is of course not Christmas. It is autumn.

It is the aid thing, the helping syndrome, you think of while you avoid the woman walking towards you. Your mother has told you many times of the great famine. And the great song. And the humiliation.

She used to say, 'There are no other pictures. We are always the famished skeletons with the kwashiorkor belly only. It's not enough, it's not right, that this is all there is to us.' Your father would reply that these were exactly the things that got your mother into trouble. Your mother would counter that at least she was still forming her own opinions.

You wonder what the pictures are now. Of people like you, here, in the camp. What will stick this time? The muddied clothes you try to keep clean but which hang drab and damp on your bodies? The queuing?

The woman arrives. She wears those practical clothes made for outdoor activities. Her jeans are too tight to have any layers underneath but her jacket is loose and has a few square pockets that look like they can hold a whole loaf of bread. You poke Mariam, who is still waiting for someone to pick up the phone on the other side. She looks up.

'Hi. How are you?'

'Good.'

The woman crouches down. It's obvious that you can't speak to anyone when you tower over them.

'I like your hair,' she says.

Mariam hangs up before her mother can answer.

You too like the woman's hair. It has just been done: the cornrow lines are sharp and the pattern is unusual. The strip of hair in the middle is twisted and falls to the sides in a straight line from forehead to neck. Mariam does yours. For some reason she took her time when she did it last. It was another sunny day, much warmer than today, and you sat outside chatting and laughing, your head between her legs as she braided it in the traditional style. She gets hers done by someone else because you're not good at it. But she doesn't do yours often. You can't really wash your hair here. It's a nightmare.

'Thanks,' you reply. What does this woman want?

She asks you how things are here. Her shoes are not appropriate for the camp. You wonder if she paid attention to the instructions given to volunteers. Her shoes are flat but dressy, good for the office. They are old but still, not practical at all.

'Difficult,' you reply. What a waste of a calm minute. You, Mariam, here. A bit of quiet while your friend comes up with more stories for her mother about how she has not been paid by the alteration service she is lending her sewing talents to before she can find proper employment. Her optimism is matched by her ability to create elaborate stories. And she can remember them: she doesn't make mistakes, draws her mother and the rest of the family into the alternate world she dreams up, distracting them from the details of her stuck-in-transit-ness.

The woman wants to sit down, you can see it. Her eyes are angling for an invitation.

'It must be hard.' She's waiting for your response. 'Here.'

Mariam is nodding but she doesn't say anything either. It's such a useless question. Your blood is starting to boil. Her five-minute concern is not going to help you keep warm at night, or leave this hellhole altogether. You will still be queuing in one line while she redoes her nappy curls in a salon at the end of next week.

'Is there any camp gossip? Any love stories?' the woman asks.

'Not really,' Mariam replies. You want to shake the woman until her hair comes loose.

'No one has time for that. Too much to think about,' you say, your lips straight, your teeth hardly lifting. She can understand. Of course she can. You don't care.

Mariam leans over and says something to you in Tigrinya. It makes you think. You pull yourself together and smile at the woman. She smiles back.

'Is that your van?' Your head jerks briefly. The mother has come out and is talking to the people who have parked next to her.

'No, my friend's there.'

'Where are you from?'

'London.'

Mariam shrugs her shoulders when you whisper to her.

'Can you take us? We'd hide in the back.'

The woman still smiles.

'I wish I could. Really, I do.'

There is no surprise, no resentment. She holds your gaze.

'Nobody would know.'

'It would be smuggling.'

Mariam is quiet, her phone resting on her chest while she follows the two of you like a close-up tennis match. Back and forth. There is more to be said about the silences than the words that leave your mouths. The way you hide your snigger – almost – so that you are ready to catch it should she change her mind.

'If the police come you just say you didn't know.'

'She is driving. I'm staying here.'

'No one has to know.'

Her voice shows you how reasonable she is. 'The baby is very young. It would be smuggling.'

'No one would know.'

'Then why do you tell me?'

Mariam is still darting back and forth between you, enthralled. The suspense.

Now the woman's friend arrives, baby in arm. 'Hello.' She is another optimist; you can see it straight away. 'She just learned this,' the mother laughs. 'Spitting bubbles.' And on cue the baby blows bubbles.

What is this? What do they want? You have other things to do. You offer her nothing: no reassuring words, no acknowledging smile.

'I'm sorry. Really. I'd love to. If I could.' The woman is waiting. She can't do this. She really can't. Surely you must agree. But your eyes are on the baby.

'Take care.' She's understanding.

Mariam offers a goodbye, but you move your head only slightly. The two women walk off, baby spitting and gurgling.

'We tried,' Mariam says. 'Next time.'

Back at the camp entrance a guy is threading another man's eyebrows outside a wooden hut, right next to the new shop. Mariam boxes you in the sides; both of you laugh.

She pulls out her phone, eyebrows raised, almost excited. She is good at this. She is a manager, a manager of affairs. Hers.

It is especially busy at the entrance to the camp. You watch the endless back and forth. People are always moving; the everyday is a complicated negotiation, a feat of endurance.

Mariam is quieter than usual. Normally she speeds ahead, getting in front of whoever is on the other side of the phone. It makes the storytelling easier. It's not a lie then, she thinks. It's just a story. When you asked her, 'How is that different?' she replied, 'Because they have not asked me. Not directly. I am just saying something that could happen.'

'It's not happening, though,' you replied, but Mariam had wiped away your concern.

She pulls you along with her. You have now passed the slip road that leads back onto the motorway. The police van is parked on the opposite side, like it has been all day, except for the time when the officers change shifts. Their uniform must be hot on a day like this, the bulletproof vests hanging on them like deadweights. Once in a while they parade in their heavy boots and their helmets with visors through the camp, down the main street and back, showing their presence. A reminder that this is merely an unspoken toleration, the staying here. The empty tear-gas canister another cue.

Mariam stands very still, doesn't say anything but 'Yes', and 'I understand' and 'I'm sorry'. Her voice is flat, no optimism, nothing.

You hold her hand and wait. As soon as the conversation finishes she drops the phone, her hand limp.

'I need to send money immediately.'

'Yes,' you say, and pick up the phone.

'You don't understand, Habena. I really have to make money. Today!'

'OK, no problem. Don't worry, it will be OK. All of this, it's just a glitch, a minor delay.'

You feel like a traitor, using Mariam's own words when her eyes are much heavier than yours and starting to leak. She turns away from the police, her back stiff.

'Her ulcer... it burst. I took too long.'

The silence between you is painful. It is too familiar: the impossibilities, the out-of-options.

'Listen, Habena, she is in hospital, but now it's even more expensive. It's not the time to tell them I am not working, that I have nothing.'

You can't say anything. It's not the time to say that you were right all along, that she should have told them.

Her eyes. You can't look at her.

'Tonight. Where the lorries park.'

You know the spot she is talking about. Other women have come back and told you about rude drivers, unwashed and sweaty. It is so bad that one truck company has started checking on their drivers; anyone caught is thrown out. The story made the rounds. You thought it was a good sign – at least someone was thinking about the women here. 'They just don't want to get caught. No one cares at all. Don't be fooled,' someone corrected you.

Even though her face is not showing it, Mariam is still optimistic. In that *everything will work out, I have a plan* way of hers.

'I'm not sure,' you say.

'What else can I do?'

Her phone is ringing again. She taps on the red symbol and calls straight back.

'Yes. Tomorrow or the day after. Western Union.'

It's colder than you expected, so you pull the hood over your head. Mariam had suggested you leave in a cardigan, with a blouse underneath, to attract business. You looked at her; she dropped it. Yes, she is your friend, but she'd better not push you too much. This is more than you wanted to do for anyone. 'Once only, for you,' you said.

It's a long walk. The lorries used to come up close to the camp but since the last police crack-down they've had to find a new spot. You walk along the street, on the grassy slope.

The parking place has a row of trees that shield it from the road. There the drivers who need to rest park before they cross the Channel. You recognise one of the women and pull your hood closer around your face.

'If you're like this, no one is going to pay you.'

There is anger in her voice. It is not directed at you, you know that. Still, it is cold. Two women are walking between the lorries, knocking at the doors, high up.

'Come.'

'Mariam, it's not the right thing.'

'Are you going to leave me hanging?'

She is not the same. Not optimistic, not the lighter of you two. She hurries towards the lorries at the other end, where the two women have already disappeared into parked vehicles.

'I will start with that one.' And she's gone. You watch her exchange a few words, but the lorry door closes again. She goes to a smaller red vehicle that looks old and dusty. No one even opens. Then, as she walks to the next one, a man jumps from the driver's cabin. A couple of minutes later he helps her climb up. The door shuts.

You are still standing where Mariam has left you.

'You all right, sweetheart?' A driver has returned from behind the bushes. His podgy hands are on his fly, pulling at the zip.

'Looking for something?'

A couple of strides and he is close to you.

What were you supposed to ask? Mariam and you have not spoken about the details. No time. She said, 'Once. Once is nothing. I need your help today. I can't go alone.' You replied, 'But I don't want any of the others to know. No one, nothing!'

'How are you?' You cough, your mouth dry.

'If you want to make some money I can help you out.'

You lower the hoodie.

'Nice!' The driver whistles, bending his torso to the right, looking you up and down. 'Must get the guys all crazy down there in the Jungle.'

You check the rest of the parking area. It's quiet.

'Where are you parked?'

He points over to a new model in silver.

'After you.'

The cabin is cramped but warm. He pulls the curtain shut behind him. You sit in the middle, he on the outside passenger seat. He starts fumbling your breast, opens the zipper to the hoodie and reaches inside. You put your hand on his.

'Money first.'

'Don't worry about that. I'll pay.' He pulls his zip back down. His hands are cold on your breast, but you are sweating. Mariam would do the same. Her mother

61

will die if she doesn't receive the right treatment, fast. She is right, you will forget it. Quickly. It will be another part of this journey. There are so many things to forget, this is not the worst of it.

You take off your hoodie, lift the top underneath, showing your body.

'Money first.'

He laughs, a bit of spit falling on your exposed tummy. The others were right. It does smell inside but he looks very eager. It won't take long. He is touching his thing through his trousers. His penis hard. You haven't even touched him.

'You're the nervous type, aren't you?' he says. He tries to soften his voice, as if you're sharing something. 'Don't worry. I never cheat a woman. I'm not that sort.'

'It's business.'

He laughs again. He doesn't stop looking at you, at your breasts, while he pushes his trousers down and takes his thing out of the fly. He reaches for your hand, places it on his penis, but you pull back and hold up your palm.

'Money or I'll leave.'

'See how far that gets you.'

He says it to frighten you. Red blotches have appeared on his face, highlighting his blond stubble. He is by the door; you are in the middle, the big steering wheel on the other side. He thinks he is clever, that you're trapped. But you're not stupid. The doors are unlocked, you watched him. 'Make sure the doors are open,' you have overheard the women say. 'That way you can leave. When you decide to.'

You have moved away from him. He reaches in his jacket, pulls out a wallet. The other hand doesn't stop, he is still rubbing his thing, his eyes fixed on your body. He flips the wallet open and pulls out a note, all with one hand.

'Here.'

'What is this?'

'You wanted your money.' He slides down in the seat, legs open, knees flopping to the sides.

You look at the ten-euro note.

'What is this? For what?'

'Did you think this was some glamour brothel, sweetheart? Ten euros, that's the price here.' His face is mocking you.

You grab your hoodie and reach over the driver's seat for the handle. He lets go of his penis, finally, and grabs you around your waist.

'You didn't think I'd take you out to dinner first, eh? Little spoiled slut, you are. You're lucky I'm a nice guy.'

He pulls you closer.

'Just a little blow job. You're a looker, you are. Beautiful, nice skin.' You can feel his breath before the stubble touches your neck.

'I'll treat you, you'll see. Might even give you another fiver, if you're nice. I'm generous like that.'

You push his arm away and climb over the seat, jump out, leaving the door open.

Mariam is just coming down from the lorry's cabin. She waves. You point the way you came and run towards the slope at the other end.

'Hey!' Behind you the guy is yelling.

Mariam is catching up with you. You pull her to run faster.

'No,' you shout. 'No! I told you. It's not right.'

It takes a while until you stop by the trees before you enter the camp.

'Sorry.' She starts crying.

'You have to tell her. Someone else will have to help.'

Mariam sits down. You let yourself fall back next to her.

It is still dark but the light from the street is enough for you to see her face. There is nothing you can do. You wipe her face. At least it will still be quiet, quieter than usual, in the camp. Maybe you'll get a bit of sleep, put some distance between yesterday and tomorrow.

Mariam starts laughing.

'That guy was lying with his face flat, hanging out of the cabin, shouting for you.'

'His thing was out, he was probably still touching himself.' You shrug. 'He thinks I'm stupid.'

You squeeze her hand.

'It's a start. But you can't make it this way.'

She opens her palm. The ten-euro note is damp from your sweat.

Paradise

No, my friend. No no no. Isaac waves a disapproving index finger and so Muhib drops his cigarette and grinds it under his boot. Even when he's down, he can't help smiling at Isaac. Such a kind guy. So serious for his age. But also funny. Of all the many people in the camp Muhib loves, he loves Isaac the most. At least at this moment he does.

Isaac lifts the kettle off the fire and pours chai into two mugs. They sit in camping chairs, hunched against the cold, sleeping bags around their shoulders, Muhib tall and lean, Isaac small as a child. Mist chills the quiet camp and smudges the far trees and the factories beyond. Settling back into melancholy, Muhib sighs, but Isaac won't let him get away with that either. He mimics the sigh and pretends to wipe tears from his eyes until Muhib laughs too.

'You will find another girl,' Isaac tells him.

'No, Isaac, not like that girl,' Muhib says. 'I don't sleep since she left. Three nights crying.'

'And smoking,' Isaac says.

'Yes, smoking and crying for Rosalina.'

'The Spanish girl?'

'Of course, the Spanish girl. So beautiful, believe me.'

'You have a big heart, my friend.'

On his zigzag trek from Sudan to France, Isaac has picked up several languages, but Urdu is not one of them and so they speak in minimal English, a few blunt words warmed with use. Neither prays at a mosque but they have Allah in common and also the school. Soon, Isaac will unlock the door and Muhib will sweep inside and round the entrance before the first classes arrive. But for now they drink chai in the donated camping chairs and dream.

Even when he's not calling her, when his voice is not literally in her ear – and, good grief, he calls often enough – Julie keeps up a conversation with him in her head. Just look at this, Dad, she's telling him, silently, as she walks down the main track into the camp. Not what you expected, right? So normal. Look – shops and cafés, families, a church.

Julie smiles at everyone she passes on the track. She read on one of the helpful Facebook pages that outsiders should smile, so she smiles at them all: smiles at the young Sudanese men, gangly-tall, whisking along on bicycles; smiles at the Eritrean women darting in and out of the café-bar, even though she can't catch the eye of any of them; smiles at Kurdish families in thick coats, big-eyed children peering out from under their hoods; smiles at the Afghan men behind the raw-plank counters of general dealers, selling headache pills, cans of Coke and Red Bull, biscuits and batteries. Traders on the new frontier.

I wish you could see this, she tells inner Dad. Seriously, you'd reconsider all those things you've been saying if you could only see how everyone gets along, how considerate people are of each other.

A woman asks Julie, urgently, where she can find a sleeping bag. Her orange lipstick is half wiped away, leaving her mouth approximate, as if blurred by motion. Julie has no idea where sleeping bags are given out, but luckily someone else helps with directions. As the woman hurries off, Julie hands her a flyer about the event in the theatre tonight. The Dome's giant beach-ball shape is drawn on the flyer so everyone can find it. Julie gives out more flyers to a group of men nearby. They don't speak much English and so, to explain what's going to happen, Julie mimes playing a trumpet, a guitar, a piano, the bongos. Then she mimes dancing. Draws quite a crowd. They applaud when she curtsies. The sun comes out. Even more people accept flyers. Smiles all around.

Well, to be honest, it's men who accept the flyers. Julie's mission is to encourage more women to attend, but so far she has seen few and actually invited only the woman with the blurred orange mouth. She would like to invite the young Eritrean women, but they scurry by so quickly. She reached her hand out to one of them earlier, a girl as petite as Julie is, her hair cresting in a grown-out Mohican, but the girl jumped aside as if Julie might strike her and that was so alarming and then embarrassing that Julie hasn't dared to approach another woman since, except to hand flyers to the husbands or sons or fathers or whoever they are.

Someone has planted a row of boulders along each side of the gravel path, about the size of human heads, and several people – well, men actually – are seated on these rocks in the sun. Julie finds one to sit on too. If it wasn't for the small crowd that clapped her over there, she'd give up right now. Really, she ought to be helping Marjorie, her tiny timid aunt, sorting donations in the warehouse with other volunteers. Really, inner Dad interrupts, she ought to be at home preparing her first university essays, instead of traipsing along with bloody Marjorie to Calais. But she's in neither of these places, doing neither of these dutiful things. Instead, she's leaning back against the wooden side of someone's shelter, stretching her legs out, tipping up the toes of her hiking boots to stretch her calves. Probably, she should be at yoga camp in Wales with her mother, but no, she's watching a man walk by in thin blue cotton shalwar kameez with a khaki anorak over the top, talking with his friend. She's watching his feet go by in worn leather sandals, like an extra from a desert film who's wandered on to the wrong set. She's wondering how he will manage in the cold that already bites from the shadows. She's addressing her father, proposing that he rethink his whole position on refugees and (please, Dad!) welcome the desert man as soon as possible to a council house of his own. With heating.

Outside the school, Muhib is practising, knee to knee with his flute teacher, a German woman with pink-dyed dreads, an orange dress and a nose ring, both of them peering down at the chords written in a book by their feet. Muhib is wearing clothes that his volunteer friends brought especially for him, stylish clothes: black stretch pants, a black and gold T-shirt and a black hoodie with sleek fat-toothed zips over the pocket. People say that Muhib is so friendly, so generous, so enthusiastic, so open. They don't say, because it's awkward, that he's handsome. And 'Muhib' is not, of course, his real name. Muhib means 'loving friend', though, so it's a good name for him.

'Tonight, you play with us?' the flute teacher asks him. 'In the Dome?'

'You think I can do that?'

'For sure, Muhib. Come on, man – one song?'

'That will be very amazing,' he tells his teacher, and she grins.

He picks up her phone and frames a photograph of her with the merry 'School' sign painted on the wall behind her head. A notice on the door requests that people not photograph the school, but that's to protect the refugees from thoughtless snappers; it's not meant for the regulars like the flute teacher who've put in the time, who've chosen the Jungle, the real troopers.

It's not a wonderful smell. But not offensive, really. Like a full laundry basket perhaps. Stale, with notes of cold wet concrete, Marjorie thinks. At her trestle table, they're sorting the shoe donations by size. Maybe that's why she's noticing the smell today, come to think of it. To one side, they pile Impossibles: broken or inappropriate shoes, including a pair of red stilettos. This morning, someone found a wedding dress packed in a trunk with other donated garments. Is that an insult? Marjorie wonders. Offloading your unwanted tat? Or might it be a romantic notion? You never know – someone might want to marry in a refugee camp, might not want to wear a bulky parka and donated trainers to their wedding, might want a white gown and even some red stilettos. In what she refers to as her middle years, Marjorie takes a more elastic line on weddings and marriage than she used to. Much to abhor, of course, in the gender inequalities of the institution, but the younger generation seem to like a wedding, even the lefties. Not to mention mad heels. Let it go.

Another thing to let go of, if she can: some guilt or doubt nipping at her gut, just under her ribs, concerning her niece. Is her brother correct? Has she brought Julie along because Julie wanted to come, being eighteen now and allowed to make her own decisions? Or is Julie here as another salvo in Marjorie's long-running war with her right-wing brother? Marjorie doesn't doubt her own true affection for the girl and doesn't care that much about her brother's opinion, but she loathes the idea of anyone – especially herself – using someone else for their own ends.

Her hands have stopped shoe-sorting. She gazes down towards the other end of the warehouse – and cavernous is the right word: it's a vast metal cave – to the shadows of people and vehicles crossing the open gates, making the sunlight flicker. New arrivals seeking signed permission slips to go into the camp. Ever more vans full of donations: sleeping bags, kids' toys, tents, food, every size of jacket, woolly hats, stout boots. Some tat, but not too much, really. And in here a hum of voices, the efficient stride of organisation, the rattle of trolley wheels over the gritty concrete floor. Marjorie smiles to herself. This comforts her, the meld of big-heartedness and discipline. A tall, grey-haired man walks past her trestle table, forehead furrowed in concentration as a young and multi-tattooed woman with a clipboard explains his task for the day.

Up on stage, the flute teacher jumps onto a chair to seek out Muhib's face in the crowd. Under its beehive hexagram panels, the Dome buzzes with voices and laughter. Muhib sees her – who can miss those pink dreads? – and slips through the crowd to the front.

'Yeah man, be close by,' she yells at him over the tuning of instruments.

Feedback squawks from a speaker as two grinning boys sprint from amps to mixing desk, bouncing on their rubber soles. Muhib nods to the guy on the xylophone, one of his Ethiopian buddies. To the side of the stage, turned away from the crowd, an older man blows notes on a saxophone and the clamour slowly dies away and it all begins.

Muhib watches the musicians, watches his teacher, watches her lips make the flautist's pout, grips his own flute, swallows. To walk up there – will he be able to do it? Will he remember the chords? Ha! Will she even remember to invite him up on stage, engrossed as she is?

She does, she remembers. First in German and then in English, she tells the audience that her student – so talented! – is going to play. 'Give a big hand, people!'

From the stage, because of the way he holds his head to play, he sees the face of one girl, a girl he hasn't met before, her hair in plaits, smiling at him, and he plays especially for her.

'My hands were shaking, believe me!' he tells her afterwards, this English girl. So sweet. Such green eyes. And her hair, which looked blonde from the stage, turns out to have red in it. 'What is that called in English?'

'Ginger,' she says, wrinkling her nose.

'Beautiful ginger!'

*

Marjorie sees him before Julie does.

'There's your handsome friend,' she says, pointing up at the restaurant window.

Marjorie has parked her van and they're heading back to the hostel. At the Afghan café in the camp, Julie had faced the door, hoping he'd walk in, hoping she'd spot him over her plate of spicy beans. And now it turns out that he's been here in town this evening instead, eating with his volunteer friends. She can hear them laughing through the open window, above Marjorie's head, sees one of them throw his arm around Muhib's shoulder. Perhaps the pink-haired flute teacher is there. Probably she's the one he's in love with.

'Do you want to go in and join them?' Marjorie asks her.

'God, no.'

How humiliating that would be, trailing around after him. With her aunt too. A pair of ginger mice.

But now Muhib has seen her and leans out of the window. 'Come, Julie,' he calls. 'Come!'

So she does. She climbs onto the railings and reaches up her hand and he and his friend lift her into the restaurant through the window, laughing, to land on her bum on the wooden floor. When she's right-side-up again, Julie shouts down to Marjorie, 'See you later!' and Marjorie waves back.

Muhib's English friend is laughing. He cuffs Muhib's shoulder.

'Oy, Romeo,' he says, 'you're the one who's meant to climb.'

Marjorie wishes she still smoked. There are times when a good novel or a sudoku or a bowl of cereal just isn't enough. Her feet throb from the long hours in the warehouse, but are they resting, elevated on the narrow hostel bed? They are not. Is she sleeping the requisite seven and a half hours before tomorrow rolls around? She is not. Is she sitting in her tracksuit on the hostel staircase, listening for sounds of her niece returning at (checking her watch yet again) 2.34 a.m.? Yes, she is. Waiting and worrying and running disaster scenarios, like any aunt might. Abduction, rape, drugs. How about too much fun? Is that a risk? What if Julie never comes back? Even in her imagination, Marjorie refuses to picture herself walking into her brother's office, refuses to script what she'd say. Well, bad news about Julie. Disappeared without a trace.

But seriously, who would she ask for help? What would she say? She can hold her own on a picket line, Marjorie can. Diminutive as she is, she can march and confront and demand with the best of them. If only she found everyday life less intimidating.

Oh, honestly, she tells herself. This is all perfectly normal. Julie's a young woman. Innocent and overprotected, maybe, but this is what youth is for: adventure and passion. It's only that I wanted her to fall in love with justice, with activism, not some boy.

One cigarette couldn't hurt. Wasn't there a vending machine downstairs?

The guy seems to be asleep in his camel coat, a thick scarf round his neck and a balaclava over his face, out here in the early sunshine, but Muhib knows he's awake and guarding the entrance of the bar, like he always does, from the opposite corner of the track. The guard pulls one mittened hand out of his coat pocket for a brotherly fist bump.

'All good?' Muhib asks him. The guy rocks his head. Could mean yes, no or maybe.

'For me,' Muhib tells him, 'all is very good, my friend.'

The guard's eyes seem to close. But he's still listening, still keeping watch. He doesn't sleep, this one, all night and well into the morning.

'For me,' Muhib says, because he must tell someone, 'this was the best night of my life.'

He seats himself on a stone beside the guard. From here, it's easy to see anyone approaching the bar, with its giant squirrel mural. It's a good position. Muhib will be able to spot Julie no matter what direction she arrives from.

But soon, instead, he sees Isaac. Muhib jumps up, eager to tell his friend about his new love, his leaping heart, their plans to meet. But Isaac is distracted.

Muhib takes his friend's anxious face in his hands.

'What is the problem, Isaac?'

Isaac smiles as if he might cry. He's leaving, he tells Muhib. The French government is offering new chances to Sudanese refugees. A rest in another town, a review of his case, possible asylum. Isaac has agreed to climb on a bus with others to be driven somewhere else in France, he doesn't know where. Some people, Isaac reports, are saying it's a trick and that they will be deported. But it's a chance, and he can't see any more chances for himself here in Calais.

When Muhib first arrived in the Jungle, a few months before, he was horrified by the dirt, the tents, the taps to be shared by so many, the stinking toilet cabins. But Isaac had lived in Darfur before Calais, had stayed in a refugee camp there from the time he was eight years old. 'For me,' Isaac told Muhib in those early days, 'the Jungle is much better.'

'It's like a heaven to you?' Muhib asked him.

But Isaac is not a romantic like his friend. He'd raised his eyebrows, looking round at the garbage holes, the mud, the plastic bags and rags entangled in the branches of dune shrubs.

'No, not a heaven,' Isaac had said. 'But still better.'

'When must you leave?' Muhib asks him now.

'Today,' Isaac says. 'The bus goes in one hour. I must put my clothes in a bag.'

'I come with you, Isaac. Let me help you, my friend.'

*

Julie walks by a tent she noticed the day before embla-
zoned with a marijuana leaf and a notice to 'Keep off
the grass' amended to read 'Keep on the grass'. But the
camp feels a lot less like a music festival this morning.
Empty. Cold. People sleep in, Julie's been told, because
their shelters are finally warming up, or because they've
spent the night trying to get on a train or a truck to cross
to England, or because – Julie smiles – they were out
in the town of Calais with volunteers last night, with
one volunteer in particular, with me. Lucky, happy me.

And now she will see him again, the wonderful Muhib.
Today is the beginning of the rest of their lives. Oh, God.
Is she going to think in schmaltzy poster captions now?
Maybe she's going to turn into one of those Facebook
over-posters: 'Share if you love someone so bad it hurts.'

Here's the bar with the giant squirrel mural on the
wall. Muhib said he'd meet her outside. Julie is a little
late, but Muhib isn't there either. Perhaps he's inside
instead? Julie pushes aside the sheet of faded African
cloth that curtains the doorway. Inside, in the gloom,
she can make out one or two figures seated at tables.
No, there are more of them. One laughs, but she can't
see his face. It's all a bit creepy. A woman stirring a
pot on a gas burner turns round and waves her spoon
at Julie, a 'get-out' motion. From behind Julie, a hand
pulls her back out onto the track. It's the man in the
balaclava and army greatcoat. He waves her on, so she
keeps going, towards the café where she and Marjorie
ate the night before.

The night before. Before.

She buys a glass of sweet milky tea tasting of spice and perches on the fruit-printed plastic sheet on the wide ledge that runs round three sides of the structure. There's only one other customer. He sits cross-legged, peeling an orange, and the spark of citrus pings the sluggish air, which feels moted with dust, fusty with body smells. Net curtains drape the high windows. And that's the door she had watched all through supper last night. She expects him to walk in at any moment. And kiss her again.

She'd asked about his first kiss. He'd shrugged. It was with a cousin in the village. So silly. And her first kiss? Oh, some boy at a party, a boy she'd never seen again. But this, Muhib had told Julie, and this, and this – these were their first true kisses. She puts one hand to her cheek, under her ear, round the back of her neck, where he'd kissed her. Her skin feels alive.

'When I come to London,' he'd said, 'I will be a new person.'

She'd shaken her head. 'Don't be new,' she'd said. 'I like you just exactly like this.' Sitting on the bench in the café, she pictures Muhib walking beside her down a London street, in Shoreditch say, his hand on the small of her back.

Now, a figure blocks the light of the café entrance, but it isn't Muhib. It's some other man, a hefty older guy. He catches her looking at him. 'Oh, hello,' he says in English, in a high fake voice. 'How are *you*? Are you well? Are you fine? Can I *help* you?'

It stings her, the mockery. She slides off the shiny plastic platform to leave. But the big man stands by the entrance with his tea, so she must walk right by him. 'You are a volunteer?' he asks her. 'I am not,' he says, pointing to himself. 'Me, I'm an *in*volunteer. You understand? I'm here, yes, but *in*voluntarily.'

He's unhappy, she sees, but still. It's not her fault, after all. 'Not our fault, not our responsibility,' inner Dad pipes up.

She slips by the big man and outside into the bright cold sunlight. The path is filling up with people, but none of them is Muhib. Why did she imagine that she'd find him so easily? Had she forgotten these crowds? They're the same people as yesterday but they seem sadder somehow. Perhaps because of Muhib's story – wound up with last night's happiness in the way Muhib wound her hair between his fingers.

'When I came to France,' Muhib had said, 'I told myself: I have crossed many countries, eleven or twelve countries – UK is nothing. I can cross to UK by closed eye. It's only a small river. I can swim across. I really did not understand.

'The first night in Calais,' he told her, 'I was wearing good clothes, looking good. There were many police and I ran from them, the police behind me, me in front, running. I had no idea where to go because I was new; it was my first time. I was so afraid to be caught again, beaten, taken to another prison. I climbed up over many fences, I climbed down, cut my hands, cut my jeans, and then there was only one fence left. I was behind the fence and there was a train, the train was being loaded and it was going to England, and I saw my dream, ah yes, going to England, but I was not able to cross that last fence.'

All around her now, on the path, Julie sees stranded people, people who cannot cross that last fence. Involunteers.

From her jacket pocket, she pulls a rumpled sheaf of flyers for the Dome. 'Come tonight,' she tells a startled man, thrusting a flyer into his hand. 'Feel free, for a few hours at least.'

She strides on, beyond anywhere she's been before, and then, randomly, into a circle: a couple of caravans, a few wooden shelters and some tents set up in a ring. Some guys are nailing boards to the frame of a new shelter, others are sorting through a pile of donated clothes with a group of volunteers in matching blue T-shirts. In the centre of the circle, two men sit on low chairs, facing each other across a lurid pink leopard-print item made of firm sponge and standing on the damp ground as a card table. The two men slap their cards down on it. One greets her in a loud voice. 'Hello!' he says, but not meanly, not mockingly like the man in the café. He says his name is Leon.

Beyond Leon's pink card table, women and children are sitting on wooden planking under the overhang of a tent, semi-secluded there. Might she get to talk with them, invite them to the Dome? How should she ask?

But Leon wants her attention back.

'You are from UK, right?' he says. 'And what message are you bringing us from Cameron? Because this place is no good. We want to leave.'

'You see?' says inner Dad. 'They all want something from you.'

Leon shouts something that Julie can't hear and rips open his shirt to show her a white plastic shell over his torso, like a gladiator's breastplate. Is it something medical or is it bulletproofing or what? She can't tell and neither can she understand why he is showing it to her. Then the cheerful British volunteers want her to take a photo, all of them together, a sea of blue T-shirts. Julie holds up their phones one by one, snapping away while Leon photo-bombs, pulling crazy faces from the edge of frame.

Walking back afterwards, no Muhib in sight and no women invited to the Dome either, Julie sees a playing card lying on the newly laid white gravel of the pathway. The Joker. She photographs that on her own phone, thinking of Leon, planning to ask Muhib who Leon is and what his breastplate might mean. Muhib will know.

Muhib can't find Julie anywhere. Not by the squirrel mural, not in the café, not on the path, not in or near the Dome or the library or the school. Watching the bus drive his friend Isaac away, Muhib had cried, and now he tastes again the nausea that burns the back of his throat when he lets himself recognise the dizzying nothing that Isaac faces and the matching emptiness all around himself. How to look away? He could hammer nails to build shelters, he could help clean the Dome, he could play his flute, he could join those boys with a football.

But no. Today, he wants to find Julie. His ginger angel.

'Always, I wanted to go to London,' he'd told her the night before, wrapping her up in his arms. 'One guy in our village went to London when I was a small boy. After a month he sent a letter. You know how it is in a village – everyone gathers round to listen to the letter. He says he is in London and it is very good there. I ask my father, "Daddy, what is London?" Of course, he doesn't know but he tells me it is a place of angels. And from that time it is my dream. London.'

'Oh dear,' Julie had said, thinking of her own father. 'Please don't expect angels.'

Muhib had turned aside, out of her embrace, to cough. A deep chest-rumbling cough. She'd stroked his head.

'Is only the smoking,' he'd told her. 'Only for now, Julie, only in the Jungle. Too much stress here. I will be a new person when I get to London.'

'What are you going to tell your dad?'

'Jesus, Marjorie, is that all that you care about?'

Julie slams the passenger door, presses the lock and

jams herself against the window, her knees against her chest, her boots on the dashboard. Marjorie is vile. Her father is vile. It's his fault. He poisons everything.

'I hate you,' she shouts as Marjorie slides into the driver's seat.

Marjorie ignores her, swipes her hair behind her ears, checks that the packet of Gauloises is in the van door and turns the ignition. Half an hour? Forty-five minutes? Then she can light up on the deck of the ferry. Except there's traffic. Honestly. Who expected Calais to have a rush hour? Will Julie leap out of the car at the traffic lights or anything daft like that?

'Why are you doing this?' Julie asks her.

'I told you.'

'You made up that shit about danger, didn't you? You just want to get me away from Muhib.'

'Seems to me he's the one who got away, darling.'

Julie kicks the dashboard. Then she bursts into tears. Marjorie is right and she hates her.

Why am I doing this, actually? Marjorie wonders. Am I protecting Julie or myself?

The motorway approaches the slip road to the Jungle and Marjorie accelerates. Julie twists round in the passenger seat to look down at the ragged encampment. Where is he, in there? Is he thinking about her? Today was grim, really, not finding him anywhere, wondering if he said those things to other girls.

Maybe I should turn around, Marjorie thinks. Poor kid, her heart is breaking.

He can find me if he wants to, Julie thinks. That English guy wrote down my email.

I probably am selfish, Marjorie tells herself. It's just so much easier when I come on my own.

She strives so hard for justice, Marjorie does, but she can't figure out what's fair here. Historical forces are so much easier to judge.

I'll find him on Facebook as soon as I get home, Julie thinks. It's a mistake, it's all a mistake. As soon as he emails me, I'll get a ticket on Eurostar and come back on my own.

She glances over at Marjorie. She wants to hurt her.

'I'll tell Dad he was right,' she says. 'They're all liars and cheats and we must keep them out of our country.'

Marjorie glares at Julie through narrowed eyes. Soft-spoken Marjorie, but she can shout when she wants to. 'Like hell you will!'

Muhib holds one foot, then the other, under a tap at the washstand. Cold air, icy water. He cleans between each toe, one after the other, a ritual as familiar as breathing. As familiar as the tiles round the well in the courtyard at home. As familiar as his mother. And his younger brothers. He can almost hear the creak of the rope winding the bucket up to the surface.

He splashes his face, twists his finger fast in each ear, shakes his head. Drops of water fly. He's hungry but he has no money, so he'll line up at the ashram for a plate of something.

Some guy is drumming outside the tent and a small crowd watches three men dancing to the drum. Two are volunteers, one is a refugee. Other volunteers are videoing the dance on their phones.

Here comes his flute teacher, a bowl in each hand – soup for herself and soup for Muhib.

'I want to ask you something,' Muhib says.

'Of course, man.'

'You will go home soon, to Berlin, right?'

She shrugs. 'Sometime I will.'

'Yes, you will go,' Muhib says. 'All the volunteers go. And you leave us here in the Jungle, thinking about you, missing you. It's painful,' he says, 'so, please, don't love us so much.'

Ghosts

He lets it be known that he leaves the camp when the trucks don't run, like at Christmas and New Year, goes to City X and gambles there, drinks and spends and screws. He holes up, they say, with some cousin or brother who lives in City X, in one of those neighbourhoods where the police don't go.

So I follow him. Why not? The first thing he taught me was invisibility. To disappear in the woods, to disappear in crowds. He doesn't even smell me. My hood up, I walk at least ten steps behind him along the streets of City X. Ghostman we call him, but he's never invisible to me. I let him get way ahead of me, but I can still see the roll of flesh along the back of his neck. I can pick out his feet in a crowd, and the way he steps, a little knock-kneed. Yes, he's weakening.

A man's greatest strength is the very same thing as his greatest weakness. So they say.

Not me, though. I say, No weakness. Period.

Gambling. Is this his weakness? He told us that he throws away thousands in a single casino night. And the others say that that's his weakness and his strength too, because what we do is a lot like gambling. Taking chances, they like to say, slapping the face of danger. Everything to lose, fortunes at stake. They talk like it's some adventure, like they don't spend hours lying on wet leaves in the dark. Like they don't shit themselves when we hear police dogs.

These boys, they talk too much. I don't talk.

And he doesn't talk.

Well. He didn't talk before, but now he's beginning to talk. That's weakness number one. Not the gambling, but talking.

Second weakness, I'm suspecting, is a woman. Not one of the women who have no money to pay him, and not one of the hookers in City X. These women are not weaknesses – he charges them, he forces them or he pays them. No, I'm thinking there's a woman who lives in City X who makes him weak.

He doesn't see me in the casino. No one sees me in the casino, not really. Girls maybe. Girls laying their soft gaze on me. I can get girls who don't owe me. I can get girls without beating them or threatening them. While he's settled in, drinking and gambling, I go with one of those girls, not for long, just outside in the alley. She isn't happy about that, about stepping into the alley, but I don't force her. She gives me soft eyes and holds my hand and follows me out.

When I walk back inside, his face is red, he's unsteady on his stool, throwing notes onto the table. I don't count any of that as weakness. Talking to me back in the camp in Calais, that's weakness.

The carpet in this place, it sucks up sound. I can hear no footstep. The ring of the slot machines by the door, of course, and voices, but not words. The speakers pour music like syrup. It's sticky in here. And warm. The opposite of the camp, I guess. But people are the same wherever. Greedy or lost or both.

The whisky I order arrives in a square-sided glass and gleams like pale gold when I hold it up to the light. Mouse would love that, anything like gold, like money, he loves. Mouse, the guy I call Mouse (no one else calls him that but me and I don't say it aloud), he counts money all the time, counting in his head when he can't be counting in his hand or on his phone, checking his bank balances. That's all he spends his money on, data bundles for his phone so he can check the piles mounting up in this account and that account. What does he think he's saving for? There's no later, Mouse, there's no villa by the sea for you or me, no boy and girl with satchels waving from the gate on their way to school, no big chair for Grandmother and no maid to help her to her feet when she wants to check the pots in the kitchen or go to prayer. Who do you think we are, Mouse? For you and me, there's only now.

I don't even like alcohol but I swallow the whisky in one gulp, my head back like a thirsty man.

When I follow him out of the casino it's not quite dawn so the streets are grey with black shadows, like smudged photographs in a textbook. His breath sends puffs of mist above his head. The heels of his leather shoes hit the pavement and echo. And still he doesn't feel me, his shadow. Not paying attention. He's Ghostman, unassailable – that's what he thinks. That's what I used to think about him too. Right now, though, he's focused ahead. She's reeling him in like a fish on a line.

We walk a long way before he stops, rings a doorbell again and again. She opens, standing in her bathrobe inside the door. She's no babe, man, she looks old to me. And fat. Not sexy fat – Mama-fat. Old, soft, kind, comfortable like a sofa. I know him. I can feel him lean to her, yearn for her.

Weakness.

From the step below, he reaches his hands to her, both hands holding on to her waist where the cord of her robe ties the big sack of her. She looks at him. Not smiling. She says something. She cups the back of his head in one hand and draws him inside her house.

Two minutes. Three, tops. I read it all.

While I'm watching the closed door, sunlight arrives. The wall was grey, like pencil shading, then suddenly it's brick orange, just the one wall facing the light.

What he taught me from day one: be feared. Long before he started telling me things, he showed me that. Strike fear. I won't lie – I did fear him, Ghostman, like everyone else feared him. Like most of them still do. And not only him: I feared many people, I feared the world. I was Fearboy, back then.

I don't remember the beating itself. I remember him unbuckling his belt.

He never hits them, though. If one of them needs hitting, we do it. Only twice have I seen him hit them. Anyone try to hit him back, we're all there to stop that person. They have to fear him. It's the only way to get them out and the only way we make money. If you mess around, we tell them, if you make a noise, if you talk to a stranger, if you vomit or scream or trip or cough, you're taking money out of his pocket and he doesn't like that. We find you a truck, you better get in it, fast and quiet. And you make it across, you better pay up.

We menace them. It's the only way.

He tells me I learned fast. He tells me it took him years to get as tough as I got in a couple of months, as mean.

Weakness, telling me that. I hate it.

Mouse says to me, 'You're like a son to him.'

'Please,' I say. 'Does a rock have a family? Does a knife?'

'Sure,' Mouse says. 'A rock's son is a stone, a sharp stone. And you're Ghostboy.'

He thinks he's funny, Mouse. Plus, he thinks he's going somewhere. He thinks he's like them, getting out of here. Mouse, you stupid fool. No destination for us, man.

You want to talk about gambling and chance? We've lost the game already, I want to tell him. If they've got your fingerprints, you've lost. If you're on a crime list, you've lost. No chance. OK, say it's a lottery, and you know what? We got the dud ticket. Our country is just plain out of date. Ten, twenty years ago, sure – asylum, refuge, future. But the roulette wheel spun round and round, and some other country's landed in the lucky spot. *Ka-ching*.

Meanwhile, they arrive in the camp with their hopes and plans and backpacks and justifications and family phone numbers. They think they've reached the finishing line after a long race, a marathon. They're from the right country, they deserve the next step, OK? Someone promised them safety. Now, they want to know if we can we get them over that last boundary.

I look into their pleading eyes. Did I ever look this way? Did I look at him with hopeful eyes?

I told him nothing. It was my uncle's friend, the man I came with, who told him stories: 'Oh, this boy. His father had to send him away. You know how it is with the village warlord – he sees your son's height, hears his new deep voice, tells you he needs your boy, he's going to take your boy to fight.'

I could tell that he didn't listen to stories like those. Even when I was cowering Fearboy, I told him nothing. I stayed near him and I watched. When I messed up, he unbuckled his belt and he was right to beat me. Some of them get wired before we go out but not me. He saw that I didn't need drugs. I sleep in the tent nearest his tent. I'm the quietest and, when someone needs beating,

I beat the hardest. And when he's sleeping, no one must wake him. To wake him, they'd have to get past me.

One woman comes to our area with her child. She has no money but, to get a chance on a truck, she must pay and she knows what that means. He told her to come this afternoon but he's still sleeping in his tent, so I give her my chair to sit on. It's a kind of holiday chair, with stripes, which I find funny and he finds funny too. 'You think this is your vacation?' he says when I sit in it, to make the others laugh. He likes to say 'vacation' in English, like we're in an American movie.

There are always desperate women like her, on the road, in the camp, even in the forest or some damn car. If he likes them, once is not enough. He passes some of them on to us. Or he has them cook or wash our clothes. I don't take them any more. I used to. I know none of them is a sister of mine but one bitch put that idea in my head. She asked me, 'Do you have a sister?' And from then on, I have none of these women. I don't need to, like I said. Girls like me and if I have to I'll pay.

The woman sits in the vacation chair with her child on her lap. She lays the kid on its back on her thighs and holds its little feet in her hands. She doesn't look at me or at any of us, only down at the kid. We're quiet because he's sleeping in his tent and no one must wake him, but she talks to her baby. Mother sounds, baby talk, smiling down at it. A boy, a girl, I don't know. Its stomach is round and its shirt rides up. She rubs the brown skin of its round belly, saying, 'Beautiful, baby-baby.' The kid gurgles back at her.

He's standing in the opening of his tent. He's been watching me watching her with the baby. I clench my fist. I want to hit something.

She looks up at him and he tips his head towards me, like: Give him the baby. So she stands up and nuzzles the baby's neck before she hands it to me. Then she walks into his tent, not looking back. He's unbuckling his belt when he pulls the tent flap closed.

The kid's eyes get watery but it doesn't cry. I know how to hold it, I used to hold my sisters, but my teeth are clenched and I would like to throw it on the ground. Here's Mouse now. He takes the baby away from me. He's on something, Mouse is – his eyes are red – but the baby's better off with him than with me.

I thought Ghostman didn't remember my story, the story my uncle's friend told, but it turns out he did, he remembered it all this time and that's why he started talking to me when he should have kept quiet. He told me it reminded him of his own story. But in those days, it was the Taliban. He told me about walking with his father to the market for food because it wasn't safe for his mother on the street. He told me his father went into the stall and he waited outside, boy he was then, thirteen years old. Five of them were patrolling and they came round the corner in their beards and robes and saw him and ran at him and grabbed him. They said he was a scout, keeping watch to warn people when the patrol approached, and they took him away and beat him.

Why did he tell me this?

Weakness.

Worse, he pulled up his shirt to show me scars.

I felt sick. I clenched my fists. I didn't look at him.

'They're still there,' he said, 'my mother and father. I send them money. I tell them I have a shop.' He laughed. 'A shop!' He punched my arm.

Mouse buys tea in the café. We're not talking, we're just sipping tea, holding the small hot glasses with the tips of our fingers and thumbs. Sipping, nodding to men we know, listening to the evening voices, figuring out who's new, what's going on. Everyone has sand in his socks – not dry clean sand like home, but this dirty wet French soil. The tea tastes right, cardamom-scented, but the sand chafes.

We know the same spies that everyone knows, the obvious ones always asking questions, but there are unlikely spies too. We can vanish in the camp, me and Mouse and the rest of us, or we can disappear in the *banlieues*, or we can live illegal in City X or City Y, but if the police catch us doing what we do, that's it. Ten years. Twenty years. So, no talking, no plans, nothing for the spies to report on. We walk out of the café, stroll down the street.

On any path in this Jungle, people are talking. Planning, striking a deal. Out here, far from ears, Mouse talks with anyone who wants to ask. People think they can trust Mouse – he has that kind of face. I'm close by, to scare them. Later, I'll report to Ghostman. He's back in his tent right now, low-profile, invisible, doing finance on one of his tablets. Six people made it over last night. Candy all round, celebration. Six times £3,000, maybe more. Most for him, plus a chunk for the driver. The rest divided by the three of us who got them to the truck, then into the truck. And some for the guy who stole the car. Have all six paid? Any follow-up needed? He's working all this out, Ghostman, in his tent.

Word gets round the camp fast. People hear about the six, those lucky six safely across La Manche. People want to talk with Mouse. He looks friendly enough but he doesn't negotiate. No, no bargains. No time for hard-luck stories. You want to go, you have to pay.

Mouse stands off the path, making a plan with three men. I'm sitting on a rock nearby. I'm making sure no one's listening in, no one's approaching. I'm like the scout in Ghostman's story about the time he was beaten and why he had to flee. Even though he wasn't actually a scout. I hate that story. I hate the weakness that made him tell it to me, the weakness that takes him to that woman in City X for comfort.

Here comes a woman a bit like her, one of the volunteers who come to help them, in her reflective bib with her heavy backpack. I'm another unfortunate refugee as far as she's concerned, so I smile back at her. Now she wants to talk with me. She thinks I need to tell my story. I shrug to show I can't understand her. She switches language. I shake my head, smiling, smiling up at her from my rock, shaking hands with all four or five of her friendly bunch. She wants to give me some flyer so I take it. Behind me, I can hear the murmur of Mouse's voice and the men's voices. Don't start handing them flyers, please, madame. They're doing business.

Please let her move on now. She doesn't. She's tugging at the straps of her backpack, trying to take it off and zip it open. 'He's so young,' she's saying. Meaning me. 'You can see how much he's been through,' she says. 'And he doesn't understand French either.'

One of the others says, 'Well, OK then.'

She reaches into her backpack and out comes a small box. It's a radio. You wind it up, she shows me how. 'You can listen to your own people,' she tells me in a loud voice, slowly. 'News from home.'

We never take donations. Ghostman's rule. But this radio is kind of cool. I mime big gratitude, tuck it in my pocket, wave at her as they move on. Finally.

But Mouse must have seen something and then reported. Back at our place, Ghostman tells me to give it to him.

'Give what?' I say. I lift my arms and Mouse frisks me. The radio's hidden by now. He finds nothing.

Ghostman slaps my face.

'We take nothing from those people,' he says. 'Ever.'

That's one of his rules for them too – anyone who wants to get across must set out from the camp in his or her own clothes, no donated shoes or coats or shirts or trousers or skirts.

He turns back towards his tent.

'Why not?' I ask. 'Why can't we take things from them?'

We never question his rules. The others wait for him to hit me again. I'm ready for it.

But he doesn't hit me. Weakness. He talks instead.

'You look,' he tells me. 'You look carefully at those trainers they bring, those boots, those jackets. You'll find something small and hard,' he tells all of us. 'Tracking devices.'

The others are nodding. 'You can't trust them,' Mouse says.

'Why do they bring old clothes?' another one says. 'It's suspicious, right? Why not real help?'

They're all nodding. Here comes a long night of stories and politics. Who started the bombing? American planes and British soldiers. And whose father died, whose brother? Swearing and smoking and then weeping for their mothers. I can't listen to it. I follow Ghostman into his tent. He hands me a parcel to give them, something for their night off: pills, weed, I don't know what. He knows I don't touch it, I don't need it. I don't listen to talk about mothers and I don't need drugs.

'Is it true,' I ask him, 'what you said about tracking devices?'

Again he doesn't hit me. He tips his head to one side. 'Might be,' he says. 'Doesn't hurt me to say so.' He laughs. 'Doesn't hurt me at all.'

It's a more powerful weapon than violence, I can see that. Better than hitting them – make sure they trust no one else.

I trust no one else. I used to trust him but he's weakening. Now I trust only myself.

It happens when I'm with a French girl. She's older than me but not old and I like her laugh. It's been a bad night. Police checkpoints on the road. Dogs in the forest. He's gone back to the camp to sleep, Mouse and the others too, but I wasn't tired so I came to this club in the town, and I'm standing outside smoking a cigarette, acting like I'm waiting to go back in, listening to the music from inside thudding through the walls, blaring out when the door opens. I light a cigarette for this girl who's stepped out. She keeps laughing when the wind blows out the lighter flame.

I ask for nothing, I suggest nothing, but when she asks me, I say OK. She's a little drunk but not too much and I put my arm around her hip when she slips. She isn't like anyone I know or anyone I knew before. I set myself a challenge: make her laugh.

It's dawn when I walk back towards the camp. The grey time. She wants to meet me again. I'm thinking, why not?

Then I see the police vans parked under the motorway at the entrance to the Jungle. They park here some days but not often this early. And seldom so many of them.

I slip by them. I know how. After all, I've been Ghostboy for two years now.

Men are standing by their tents, and outside shelters and cafés. I keep to the shadows, I listen to the talk, but these guys don't know anything. Police marching, they say, not searching tents, not fanning out across the camp, they tell each other, just marching directly that way.

They wait. I wait.

We hear the tramp of boots. This is sleeping time in the camp but not this morning. Everyone is awake. Here come the police. I swallow because I think I know what I'm going to see and my stomach is twisting.

His wrists are manacled. His head is bare. More police stride in front and behind and to the side of the two holding his arms, and they all have rifles at the ready, as if someone might try to rescue him. Everyone falls silent as they pass. He's the only one they take.

There's a clamour afterwards, like their boots stirred up a wave of voices. Around me, people are talking shit. Oh, this one knew him, that one remembers him, they all hate him but – oh, God – what will they do now? Others will surely charge more now that he's been caught. How did the police know exactly where to find him? Did one of his people sell him out?

I haven't slept for many hours, maybe two days and nights, and suddenly I'm dizzy. I lean against the wooden shack wall. I don't want to think about them bursting into his tent. I don't want to imagine him, right now, being shoved into a police van. I try to remember the girl, the French girl, her laugh and her hair falling forward over her eyes.

'So this is where you are,' says a voice behind me.

It's Mouse. I look down at his feet. He always sleeps with his trainers on, in case he has to run.

'Mouse,' I say. I forget for a moment that I never call him that out loud, but he doesn't say 'What?' or ask me why.

'There's people,' he says, 'who want to speak with Ghostman.'

I nod.

'So,' he says, 'I'll bring them to your tent.'

Lineage

Enitan is hammering. It's supposed to become what he calls the hospital. Somewhere dry and sheltered. Wooden pallets fixed together, more solid than the canvas of the tents and the tarpaulins. The tent where Enitan sleeps is there, right next to the wood and his tools. On the other side of the clearing, by the spacious shack, a queue has formed. It is drizzling.

This queue breathes: men are chatting and pushing forward in a friendly way, checking out what's happening inside the tent. A woman with blonde curls that fall into her face when she tilts it, which she does often, is attentive and fast-working. The other barber is a man with tight-cropped curls. He frowns a lot, taking a step back, rocking on his heels, hand still on his customer's head, brushing away stray clippings, tousling the hair into the right shape.

Ramzi is standing in line with the others. Farrukh recognises his slumped posture from when he saw him with his mates at the water taps yesterday. That's when he found out his name.

'You from the UK?'

Ramzi nodded. There wasn't a reason not to answer – Farrukh didn't want anything from him: We're just killing time. We're all here, innit, not like one of us got a golden ticket. Ramzi didn't look at him, though.

Eventually one of his mates said, 'Today not good. You from UK?' He pointed at Farrukh.

'Yeah, man.'

'He too, from Newcastle.' He pointed at Ramzi. 'Why you here?'

'I need to get back, man.'

'He too.'

Ramzi was detached, not engaging at all. Like the guy said, it wasn't his day.

'He is Ramzi. From Afghanistan but also from UK.'

Farrukh nodded and left. He could always wash a bit later. No need for bad energy because some guy was having an extra bad day.

Ramzi still looks depressed. He does need a haircut; really needs it. His black strands are tied at the back but some fall out over his face. He can't pull this one off, not this bloke; the long strands pull him down, making his face even sadder.

Farrukh tries again. Would be rude not to.

'Hi.'

'You all right?'

'Getting your hair done?'

'Yeah. You?'

'Yeah.'

'About time.'

'Yeah.'

Ramzi's shoulders are up by his ears, maybe because of the drizzle, maybe because he's cold, maybe because of *fuck off*.

'You from Newcastle?'

'Yeah.'

'Why you here, then?'

Farrukh isn't in the mood to beat around the bush, doesn't have that sort of patience today.

'Long story.'

'Yeah, same.'

The hammering is getting louder. Enitan's friend has joined, a skinny dark man with a metallic blue jacket. They are fixing slats to the frame. It's starting to look good. The corner poles are in place and now the sides are going up one pallet slat at a time.

Farrukh turns to them. 'Nice place you got there.'

But Enitan is distracted.

'Nice place,' Farrukh repeats.

'It's not for me.' Doesn't look like Enitan is in the mood to give him any face time.

'Why not?'

'Because I have a place. This is going to be a hospital.'

'Yeah, you've said.'

'You asked me before?' Now he's got Enitan's attention.

'No, I heard. You told someone else.'

Enitan is checking Farrukh out, eyes lingering. His phone rings and he straightens up, answers. A young white man with blond dreadlocks comes up from the street with a roll of nylon string in his hand. It's all different colours: red, blue, green and yellow.

'Hey, can I have that string?' someone from the queue shouts.

The dreadlocked guy laughs and shakes his head, then points at Enitan. 'Sorry, but it's for him.' He is aware that he's carrying a rare commodity, something too useful for people not to try and barter for.

Enitan hands the hammer to his friend, steps out of the wooden frame into the mud and puts his hand up, asking the dreadlocked volunteer to wait while he's on the phone.

Farrukh hasn't so much but blinked, he's following every move.

'That guy is connected; he can get anything.'

Ramzi is lost. What is the point here exactly?

'His new place?'

'No, he's making something for the camp. First aid, classrooms, something else I forgot.'

'Why?'

'Someone has to. It's good, innit.' Farrukh is tense.

'I can feel the water underneath my sleeping mat when it rains.'

Farrukh is still watching Enitan, who is making big gestures while he talks.

'You gotta make yourself a better place, man. Find some wood. Anything. You can't just give up. Ramzi is your name, right?'

'Yes.'

'Ramzi, that guy there, he is, like, busy. Watch him. If you want to make it here you gotta get busy.'

Ramzi's frame tightens. 'How long have you been here?'

'Five weeks. Supposed to have been a quick stop. I lost my temper. Wasn't supposed to be here.'

'No one is supposed to be here,' Ramzi says.

Farrukh is surprised. Didn't look like Ramzi had it in him, this talking back.

A new family arrives. It's obvious by the way they look around the clearing, they have no idea where anything is. The volunteer who is leading them stops, points to the barber. The two women are led away by the tall man, whose hoodie has *One Love* written over its back. The young boy follows his mother, his hands holding on to the outside of her legs to help him spin around.

The men have joined the line.

'I have been living in the UK from time. Already had grant to stay and all.'

'Yeah.'

Farrukh turns to the new arrivals.

'You have tents? They give them out in that caravan over there.' The pink van is parked on the other side of the clearing.

'They make a place for us.'

Farrukh approves. 'That's good. Your family?' The other man, who looks like a younger version of the father, is barely in his twenties.

'Yes.' The father introduces himself. 'We're from Sinjar, Kurds from Iraq.'

Farrukh turns back to Ramzi. 'I'm just saying, 'cause I have seen you and you don't look like you're in good shape. You need to get busy. Don't let it get you down. Just saying. No offence meant.'

The small boy comes running from behind a tent. His trainers soak up the damp through the holes in the soles. Mud splashes up his legs. He is giggling, running fast, his father chasing after him.

Ramzi is on snooze, hasn't said anything, but Farrukh keeps talking. 'I shouldn't be here. Left ages ago, like when I was really young, innit. Been up in Leeds. Now I'm stuck here, can't get back.'

Farrukh wants to chat, but Ramzi is stalling him like a clutch stuck in neutral.

All of a sudden Enitan shouts, 'Wait for me, just one minute.' He jumps down the rise between the clearing and the camp road beneath and walks off with the dreadlocked volunteer. As if on cue, Enitan's skinny friend puts down the hammer, pulls a piece of tarpaulin over the wooden frame, sits underneath and wraps his arms around himself, the blue of his jacket bright.

The queue is getting smaller; only the new family,

Ramzi and Farrukh are left. The woman with the blonde curls steps out of the tent.

'Quick break.' She smiles.

Ramzi does a good job, his smile is convincing, his face no longer looks like he has gum disease.

'You can go first,' Farrukh offers.

'That is nice of you.' Ramzi is not impressed.

The father is throwing his little son high up in the air, catching him, arms outstretched. The sun breaks through the trees at the back of the clearing. The boy is happy and shrieking.

'Do you remember when you first arrived?' Ramzi asks.

'In Britain?'

Ramzi nods.

'Of course.'

'I mean the first thing that happened.'

'Yeah, I do.'

'First British person I met was a policeman. Opened the lorry and said, "Welcome to England." Then they took me to prison.' Ramzi says it like it wasn't even him, like it's some random piece of information that doesn't belong to him.

Farrukh laughs. 'That's what they do. How old were you?'

'Thirteen.'

'Did you shit yourself?'

Ramzi is back on minimum exertion, no reaction. Maybe Farrukh is pushing his luck. He is shifting from one foot to the other – it's cold, that drizzle has made him uncomfortable. But he can't leave Ramzi here. He has to wait, see what the barber can do with this sad face. They are both good but the guy knows a thing or two about changing the men with a new cut.

'I was thirteen. Some guys I knew died in a car boot. I was lucky. I was in a lorry, there was air,' Ramzi offers.

'I know what you mean. I shat myself. Like proper. I was only fifteen, innit.'

'Yeah.'

The little boy is running around again, his arms spread wide, turning and making the noise of a plane engine.

'How old?' Farrukh asks.

The father holds up four fingers.

The woman barber stubs her cigarette out on a stone.

Ramzi turns to the younger relative. 'Go. You just arrived. You got lots of things to do.'

The male barber is now available too. Ramzi and Farrukh both nod towards the father, catch each other, look away. The father puts his hands together in prayer, bows.

'How long have you been here?' Farrukh says.

'Two months,' Ramzi replies.

Enitan is climbing back up the mound from the road.

'What is it with you and this guy?'

'Nothing.' Farrukh's tone is sharp. 'I just find him, don't know, he is like always doing something.'

Ramzi scoffs. 'Just now you told me to get busy. Which one is it?'

But Farrukh is again fixed on Enitan, who is standing in front of the frame, hammer in hand. His friend is still squatting underneath the plastic, head hanging over his bent knees.

'Doesn't look like he wants to work any more.' Farrukh's voice is high now.

'He's tired,' Enitan replies. He says it like *I'm tired of you.*

He holds a piece of wood, fishes some nails out of his jeans pocket, props the wood up with his elbow and uses his left hand to hold a nail, then begins to hammer with his right hand.

'You have a lot of tools.' Farrukh has moved closer. 'I might want to borrow some.'

'I don't give them out. If you need to you can use them here, but they can't leave this place unless I'm there too.'

'How am I going to use it here? I'm on the other side of the road, Iranian section.' Farrukh is standing with his hands in his jeans.

Enitan does not reply. Hammering seems to be his number-one priority.

'You got to be kidding me? Just let me borrow them, mate.' Farrukh's winding him up.

'Sorry, can't give them out.' Enitan places a couple of nails between his teeth.

'Why not?' Hiding his anger isn't part of Farrukh's repertoire, but Enitan is all Zen and calm, starting on the next slate.

The young Kurdish man is leaving the barber's tent with the sides of his head shaved.

Ramzi taps Farrukh on the shoulder.

'He's full of himself,' Farrukh snorts.

'Not really, mate. Would you just give away your stuff? Maybe if you asked a little nicer.' Ramzi seems to have all the insights. Suddenly.

The Kurdish father is leaving the barber's tent too.

Farrukh wants to shout over to Enitan, say that he needs the tools, but his throat is on fire. His fingers turn white from squeezing them inside his pockets.

The woman barber calls, 'OK, ready.'

Ramzi gives Farrukh a little push.

'I'll wait here if I'm finished first.'

'Nowhere to go anyway, is there?'

After, Ramzi catches Farrukh walking off, sliding down the mound towards the road. Enitan is still hammering in the background.

'Why did you talk to me?'

'Why not?'

'You made such an effort. Many guys to talk to here.'

'You already know England, innit. Not everyone speaks good English here. Ever noticed?'

Farrukh stops in the middle of the path.

'I just wanted to talk. Chat, you know.'

'Why are you here?'

'My mother is sick. I wanted to see her. I came here to get smuggled back to Iran. Can't really go with a visa, can I, while I'm waiting for my indefinite stay.'

'I see.'

'You see what?' Farrukh's head is jerking around.

'I understand.' Ramzi pauses for a second, then starts again. 'OK, you're fed up with me now, but you the one that bugged me. Make up your mind next time.'

He calls after a guy and trots to catch up with him. In less than a second Farrukh is beside him.

'I'm not annoyed with you. Just this place.'

He holds out his hand. Ramzi isn't in the mood but Farrukh keeps his hand there, steady, until Ramzi shakes it.

'Why are you so depressed, man?' Farrukh is pretending it's not been him, doom and gloom all afternoon, ready to burst.

'Why? I'm stuck here.'

'We're all stuck here. It's not for ever.'

'How do you know?' Ramzi is waving for his friend, further up, to move on.

'I'm waiting for my papers to go through. I shouldn't have left Leeds. I even tried to get back, went to the police here and told them everything so they could deport me to England.'

The laughter breaks out of Ramzi like he has been waiting for a good one for a while. 'How did that work out for you?'

'They said it's not their problem.'

'You crack me up. You pretend to be all smart and stuff, that you know how to do this, and you go to the police?'

'I know.'

Embarrassment isn't even the word. Everyone has told Farrukh this. Everyone. Police and refugees, not a great combination here. He was lucky they didn't drive him far away and release him in the middle of a field somewhere.

'My mother begged me not to come, but I was already here. I had to do something. Not my brightest moment, I know.'

Farrukh thinks about how he left. Long time ago. The walking to Turkey. Then in a lorry, being handed over from one smuggler to another, until he was finally in England, at the police, then foster care. All went well, over the years, kind of, if not for his little problem. His temper. Always getting him into trouble because he can't wait for the fog in his head to clear. His indefinite stay was practically a formality, yet here he was, squatting like the new arrivals.

'If I hadn't lost it, I wouldn't be here. Not your typical story. A lot of the guys think I'm proper slow.'

'I don't.' Ramzi's answer ricochets. 'I understand. Haven't seen my mother, or anyone from my family, for seven years.'

'Hard times, man. Hard times. Why are you here in the first place?'

'I turned eighteen. They refused my case. Been living on the low until a few months ago.'

Farrukh motions down the path. 'Let's have a tea in the Afghan café. Don't worry, I have money. Not much, but enough to get warm.'

The café is crowded and noisy. Men sit cross-legged in little groups on a wooden seating platform covered in waxed cloth. Bowls of sugar are standing at equal distances. The floor is filled with shoes. The air is thick with smoke.

Farrukh buys spiced teas and they sit down on the edge of the platform.

'Do you speak to your mum?'

Farrukh blows into the hot plastic cup.

'I haven't spoken to her or my sister in seven years. Don't even know where they are.'

'What?' Farrukh turns, the thin waxed cloth shifting with him as he moves.

'I have nowhere to go in Afghanistan. Nowhere.' Ramzi points to the door. The blond volunteer, the one with the dreadlocks from earlier, greets the chef, who is busy with a big pan of rice.

'Used your clothes line?' Farrukh can't help himself. The volunteer is lost.

'Your string. The plastic,' Farrukh says.

'Ah yes. You needed some.' The volunteer laughs. 'It's very popular here.'

'It is. Where did you get it?'

'I bought it.'

'I see.' Farrukh knocks the tea back. 'Another one?'

Ramzi's glass is half full.

'Sit with us?'

The blond guy joins them, happy for the company.

'Which part are you staying in?'

'Iranian,' Farrukh replies.

'Afghan area.'

'I'm staying with some Sudanese men. Brothers really.' He leans forward and extends his hand. 'Sébastien.'

Ramzi shakes Sébastien's hand. 'Ramzi. And this is Farrukh. How long have you stayed in the camp? You're French, right? Your accent…'

Sébastien laughs. 'Yes, a white man, French, staying with his Muslim brothers. They're teaching me about our faith.'

'That's interesting.' Farrukh looks like he wants to nap.

Ramzi's eyes widen. 'You're Muslim?'

'I converted last year.'

'Here?'

'No.' Sébastien smiles now. 'I converted before. I came to volunteer and became friends with some of the people here. They invited me to stay. My brother, the one I'm staying with, he is waiting for his claim to go through. Then he will come and live with me and my family. Until then I stay with him.'

'You are staying here? In the Jungle? Why?' Farrukh is stunned.

'To learn. My family is not Muslim. They don't under-stand. Here I can be in my faith and with my brothers all the time. They're teaching me to be a man. A Muslim man.'

'OK.' Farrukh looks like he is losing his faith. 'So, you mean, you're sleeping here, although you have a home in France, a real home?'

'Yes.' Sébastien's face is rosy from the condensation in the café. He looks like a little boy, open and trusting and proud.

'There is nowhere better for a white man like me to learn about what it means to be a Muslim than here.'

'How?' Ramzi is on high alert now.

'The Jungle is like a laboratory.'

'A what?'

'You have to live with people, get along. Look at the Muslims. Here we have Sunnis and Shias living side by side, helping each other even. Some of them left their countries because it was dangerous for them there. They decided, I will not live like this, I will go and find a better place where I can survive, where I can build a life for me and my family. When they arrive here they are even closer to each other than at home.'

'You're deep, man.' Farrukh is becoming restless again. His legs are twitching.

'They come here to this awful place and they make a life for themselves. Try to keep their dignity. I learn so much from everyone here. About Islam, about life. Some told me that they feel they are cowards because they left, they didn't stay and fight. But they are real men, they are brave.'

Farrukh can't sit still any longer; he jumps up.

'Another tea?'

Sébastien is quicker. 'Please, I will.'

He's back with three steaming cups in a minute.

'You work with that guy all the time?' Farrukh's foot is scraping along the floor.

'Who, Enitan?'

'Don't know his name. The guy this morning.'

'I help out where I can.' Sébastien slides onto the platform, crosses his legs, puts the tea down in front of him. 'And you, how long have you been here?'

'Two months,' Ramzi says.

Farrukh is watching a guy at the entrance. He is limping in, on crutches, one of his legs in a cast.

'Did you come here from Afghanistan?'

'No.'

Ramzi is leaning back to get comfortable. Whatever valve was keeping him shut earlier is open now, here in the warm shack. It's gushing out freely, his story. The story of his father.

'They even sent us a letter, the Taliban. My father had been a commander during the Soviet–Afghan war. That's why they wanted him. He said, "I have my family now, I already fought." We had land, we didn't need the money. We were living a happy life.'

Farrukh checks him from the side. The barber did a good job. Above the temples the hair is clipped back, the top falls to the sides, wavy. The face appears rounder this way, not as pulled to the ground as before.

Ramzi's eyes are in full motion, as if he can still see it all.

'One day I returned from a friend's house and they had taken my father. Kidnapped him.'

Sébastien's whole body is acknowledgement, listening.

'They wanted to show the villagers what happens when they ask you and you keep refusing. We don't know, up to today, if he's dead or alive. We heard that he was killed by the Taliban. But we don't know.'

They all drift off. Farrukh is thinking about his own father.

'I had no option. The Taliban came for me too. My mum told them I wasn't home. But she knew they would eventually find me. So she told me to leave and get to the UK.'

Farrukh puts his hand on Ramzi's shoulder. Ramzi smiles at him, his eyes narrowed. Farrukh pats him on the back.

'I'll be right back, need to take a leak.'

It's dark but Farrukh knows his way around. The sporadic fires, for cooking and to keep warm, help.

Here is the mound that leads to the clearing. It is quiet at this end of the camp. Mainly family tents. Farrukh climbs over the rise and waits. The barber's shack stands tall; its white walls are visible even now. Enitan's place is not that obvious, it blends into the night. He steps carefully until he touches one of the corner poles with outstretched hands. His breathing is quick. Weird. He didn't run, he didn't even rush down here, there is no reason. He takes a few mouthfuls of air, looks around. Tents and shacks are sticking out against the night sky. The air feels good after the stuffy café. He moves his foot along the bottom of the construction to the opening that will become the door. It's easier to step over there. He doesn't need anything in particular but he knows he needs something, here and now.

His phone shines a dim light onto the grass in the middle of the hut-to-be.

'What is it you want?'

The voice surprises him. He stumbles and falls onto his backside.

Enitan's friend is sitting in almost the same position that he did in the afternoon. Only now he is inside the blue tent that matches his jacket. A torch is switched on, throwing his shadow against the thin walls.

'What is it you want?' he repeats. He looks as tired and beaten as earlier, opening the zipper. But he doesn't look shy.

'Nothing.' They stare at each other while Farrukh backs away slowly. 'Thought I'd lost my screwdriver here earlier.'

'You did not have a screwdriver. You said Enitan has to give you his stuff.'

'Borrow.'

'He said no.'

'My mistake.'

'Don't come back here.'

'Or what?'

Farrukh can't help himself.

Enitan's friend comes out of the tent. Farrukh scrambles down the rise, his head pounding. Some guys, so full of themselves, no consideration, just trying to get ahead themselves. Not like Enitan bought the stuff himself. It didn't really belong to him.

Ramzi and Sébastien are still talking. A couple of others have joined them. There is a plate of food between them. Farrukh is sweating. He brushes off the grass from his trousers, his fingers shaking. Ramzi introduces him to the new crowd that has joined them.

'Farrukh? Old-fashioned,' a plump guy observes.

'Yep. Mum named me after some poet.'

Farrukh's eyes focus on the entrance to the café; he's pulling at his collar.

'You know any of his work?'

'No.' Farrukh is still avoiding him. 'Like you said, old-fashioned.'

'Come on,' the plump guy challenges. 'You must know something –'

Boom!

The air splits. An explosion rattles the tent. For a second there is nothing, just silence, then the shouting starts, the sound of falling debris. Everyone runs outside and down the street towards the flames.

*

'Careful, careful.'

People run with water and help to pull whatever they can out of the fire. It's busy, consuming everything in its way. There are orange flames: they reach into the sky, jumping to a nearby tent.

'No one is hurt so far, but watch it, everyone.'

People are shouting and scattering the burning things to starve the fire. Farrukh walks back to the café. The cook returns behind the counter.

'Too dangerous here.'

'Shit happens.'

'Let me know if the fire spreads. I'm taking care of the food here, otherwise I would be helping.'

'There are enough people. Nothing you can do anyway. Already contained.'

'Dangerous place. This time we're lucky.'

'Guess so.'

Farrukh sits back down. It's completely empty inside. The cook hands him another tea.

'Don't worry. No one is hurt. Tomorrow it will be repaired, you'll see.'

'Sure.'

It takes a while until the others return. The plump guy comes straight over and pats Farrukh on his back.

'Always fires, so easy here.' He sits down next to him. 'A poem would help us all now, you know.'

'Don't think so. Told you it was my mum, I don't even know nothing.'

'Come on.' The café is filling up with smoke again. 'For us. For tonight.'

Farrukh is not going to make a fool of himself, not here, not now. Ramzi and Sébastien arrive. Ramzi is all over the place, his eyes wide open again.

Farrukh shifts on the platform. 'Fire out yet?'

'Almost.'

The plump guy tries again, but Farrukh doesn't look like he is going to change his mind. So the plump guy stands up, raises both arms, then lowers the left hand down on his heart. His voice carries over the noise in the small shack. Words about the sky, and descending, abandoned, into exile.

'Do you know it?' Ramzi whispers to Farrukh. 'It's that poet he was talking about.'

'Probably.' Farrukh leans closer. 'My father disappeared as well. Just went missing. No one knows where.'

'Why?'

'The things he said. I was young, I don't know everything. But in my country you can't even change your religion. That's why my mum doesn't want me to come.'

The plump guy is stepping forward, his eyes closed now, making a show of it. The men laugh but their eyes are fixed on him. His face is full of it. Dramatic pauses. These things resonate, the memories, fate, all that brought them here. Especially when the longing is heavy in each word. Exile.

When he stops, the last sentence hanging in the air, the whole shop starts clapping. Sébastien looks even younger, his face glowing.

'What happened? You were gone for a while.'

Ramzi is acting like they're good friends now. The plump guy shakes a fist and thanks his audience.

'Well done. My mum would be proud.' Farrukh raises his palm and they slap their hands together.

Ramzi can't leave it, leans over again. 'Where did you disappear to?'

The men go back to their little groups, mood raised. A poet, here, now, in between all the smoke, inside and outside.

It's not like they are friends, really. He doesn't owe Ramzi anything. Least of all an explanation.

'To take a piss, like I said.'

Oranges in the River

I. THE SAME SKY

Refrigerated trucks are the best bet. If the smuggler is skilful, if he can open the padlock to let them in and then close it again so that no one can tell it's been tampered with, then the police are less likely to check a freezer than any other kind of truck. But fate is frowning down on Dlo with heavy eyebrows. The freezer door isn't even open yet and Dlo's breath is already seizing up, coming in quick, shallow gasps.

'With my luck,' he says, 'the driver will lower the thermostat. We'll die.'

'You'd rather live in the camp for ever?' Jan asks him.

He wants to shout but they must murmur. If the smuggler hears them, they're in trouble. And if the truck drivers hear them, the whole night is a bust.

'Trust me,' Jan says into his friend's ear. 'How's my luck, Dlo? Tell me. My luck is good, right? So trust me.'

He holds Dlo's skinny shoulders in his big hands He grips them through to the bones. His luck is strong like his hands are strong. He'd carry his friend if he could. He'd breathe for him.

In the four hours they've been waiting, Jan has kept
still while the cold has risen like a river, icing his wet feet
and climbing his ankles, then his calves, then his knees.
Jan wants to stamp feeling back into his feet but he's
learned to shiver instead, to make no sound. Beside him,
Dlo trembles. Fear and cold, both, Jan thinks.

Clouds cover the sliver of moon. They can hear rather
than see the smuggler at work on the padlock, the faint
clicks of the screwdriver on metal. They wait for the
louder clank of success as the shackle releases. Instead,
one of the smugglers loses his grip on the wrench and
it clatters against the metal door. A trucker shouts out.
The smuggler is on his feet and gone, sprinting with his
partner into the darkness. Jan, Dlo and the others dart
away too, taking different directions, truckers shouting
behind them as they crash through the wet bushes.

Arrive together, flee on your own.

There's a kind of freedom in moving at last after the
hours of waiting, the beat of blood in Jan's ears, the
thud of his feet on the ground, but it never lasts long,
this exhilaration. He runs and runs, as he has on so
many other nights, until he must stop. Where is he? No
compass, and he dare not switch on his mobile for GPS.
The rest of the night stretches ahead of him, endless,
empty of anything but cold and confusion. Where's the
damn moon, his only clue? He listens for cars or trains
or people. As he trudges along, fists jammed into damp
pockets, he tries the usual memory games, but they're
fading with overuse. He can't conjure up the idea of

sunshine and heat – they're some fantasy he once read about somewhere. Like home. Like Hasakah. While his feet walk France, he's remembering the neighbourhood square. Himself and Dlo, fourteen years old? Fifteen, sixteen? Half a lifetime ago. They're out after midnight, free under the street lights, sprawled on the tiered seats, replaying Real Madrid's latest match move by move, waving their arms, jumping up to celebrate. Teenage Dlo munches on cashew nuts, offers the bag. Jan shakes his head. Grins in the French dark and shakes his thirty-two-year-old head. Dlo and his cashews.

At last Jan sees the fierce white fences that line the railway tracks and the road to the ferries, spotlit in the dark winter dawn. In the shadows below the motorway, the camp. He and Dlo often laugh about this moment, finding the camp after a night's wandering, the relief of being back in this sorry collection of tents and huts.

'It's like we found Canada!'

'Hello, New York!'

Will Dlo already be back in their tent, trying to fall asleep in his wet clothes, or is he, Jan, the first to get home and Dlo still walking?

At the edge of the camp, Jan switches on his mobile to read the anxious texts from his mother. She doesn't sleep until she hears from him. He and Dlo, fully night creatures now, will sleep much of the day and into the afternoon, and Jan hopes his mother can too.

He types: *I am safe, Mama, under the same sky. Go to sleep now.*

II. BONJOUR!

The truck is parked off the road, in a lay-by beside a river, almost half a kilometre away from the place where the truckers eat and sleep. Ideal. But it's another freezer truck and Dlo's panic is rising.

'It's not a meat truck,' Jan tells him. 'It's not meat and it's not fish, so it won't be too cold.'

'Minus four or minus six maybe,' says one of the others, 'but not minus ten or minus thirteen.'

They speak a little louder than usual, the five men standing in the shadows while the smugglers open the truck.

'And Dlo, if it's too bad, if you can't breathe, we just bang on the side,' Jan says. 'Right, guys?'

The others nod. The smugglers aren't Kurdish but one understands enough. He turns from the truck door to threaten Jan.

'You bang,' he says in English, 'I lose money.'

Jan says nothing.

'You make me lose money,' the smuggler says, 'I'll find you.'

He's young, this guy, skinny, maybe around twenty-two years old. He doesn't need to make his threat more specific. Everyone in the camp has heard stories about a fool who crossed a smuggler, or one who didn't pay – how the smuggler found the double-crosser in the camp and beat him, how another smuggler found the family of the man who didn't pay and forced them to hand over double. You hate them and fear them, the smugglers, and you have no chance without them. Smugglers got Jan and Dlo from Iraq and Turkey – no way to cross directly from Syria into Turkey, the border guards shoot you if you try – and then, after days in Istanbul and Izmir, and days crossing Turkey, it was more smugglers who got them into the dinghy and across the sea to the Greek island, a gang of them, Kurds together. And a smuggler was a priority when they reached Calais all those weeks ago, Jan and Dlo. Other refugees showed them where to go to get a tent, where to line up for a coat, for boots, for a meal, but no one wanted to introduce them to a smuggler. Suspicion clouded the air. Who was a spy for the French police? Who dared risk a smuggler's wrath? No one at first and then, finally, Walat.

Dlo calls him Fearless Walat, with some envy.

'Fuck the smugglers,' Walat said. 'Come.'

They followed him through the camp, quiet with their own doubts and fears. Who was this guy, with his unrealistically dapper clothes, smoothing the flick of his jet-black pompadour as he sauntered down the dirt track? Striding behind Walat, Jan set his shoulders back and lengthened his pace, clenching his fists, with Dlo almost keeping up. Walat smoked, all nonchalance, as he led them to the far edge of the camp, to the crest of a small dune. Below, they could see several men moving in an encampment under the trees. Fearless Walat flicked the butt of his cigarette over his shoulder and called out, 'Sir! Sir!'

A man approached them.

'These guys are looking for a smuggler,' Walat told the man.

The nerve of Walat. The man said they must wait. When he came back, he gestured for them to follow him to the opening of the leader's tent, there in the centre of his undercover empire. He's safe there, the smuggler kingpin, invisible as a refugee or a migrant, with his forces around him. Dispatching drivers to earn his money and take his risks, drivers who'll be locked up if they're caught with a carload of 'illegals'.

The price was high. Jan stared directly at the smuggler king as he named it, making sure not to glance at Dlo beside him. They had enough left, but only just, in the accounts in Syria. Every possible family asset sold off to feed those accounts, to fill them with enough money to transfer to the smuggler once the sons reached UK.

'The police and immigration officials are stopping more vehicles these days,' Walat told them later, 'and searching with dogs and flashlights. They hold a piece of equipment,' he said, 'against the side of a truck to detect human heat.'

Dlo walked heavily back into the camp, weighed down by his father's sacrifices, but Jan squared his shoulders and drove himself forward, drilling towards the future, relentless and unstoppable. He recognised something in Walat. Admired him. Fuck the smugglers! Fuck the French! Fuck this lousy Sleeve of sea!

Now the skinny smuggler, the padlock shark, has the door of the truck open. Even colder air wafts out of the freezer into the cold night. They all stare up at the wall of boxes in there. One smuggler leaps in and starts throwing boxes out for his accomplices to hoist into the river running beside the road. A box splits open as it lands, spilling oranges that roll out along the tarmac and into the bushes. Dlo picks one up and slips it into his pocket. Like a man who isn't going to climb into a truck full of oranges, like a man who isn't going to sit surrounded by thousands of oranges for many hours. Like a man who needs just one orange for his thirst.

Jan and the others pick up the loose oranges and throw them into the river. There go boxes, floating downstream under the moon. There go oranges, bobbing one by one in the current and rapidly out of sight. Irrigated and fertilised, then picked, graded, wiped shiny and packed – in vain. To float away down some French river and then what? Rot, probably.

Jan follows Dlo and the three other men into the cave the smugglers have made in the midst of the orange boxes. He can't allow fear. Dlo has taken all the fear available and in turn he, Jan, must carry all the courage. But his jaw is rigid as he takes his last breath of the open air. Then the heavy steel slab closes them into utter dark. He puts his hand forward to feel the cold metal of the door in front of his face. He imagines – because he can't hear – the skinny smuggler replacing the padlock. Beside him, Dlo takes abrupt sniffs of air. The freezer is sealed, airtight, and Dlo will be calculating again and again the volume of the space and how long they have before the oxygen runs out.

'We'll bang on the sides if it gets dangerous,' Jan reminds him.

'We will if we have to,' says one of the others.

'Fuck the smugglers!' Jan says.

'We'll tell the smugglers that the police stopped the truck,' says the other guy.

But would anyone hear them? Jan wonders. If it comes to that, banging on the insulated sides of the truck might not save them. He rubs his cold fist in circles on his chest. Beat, heart. If this isn't worse than staying in Syria – and so far, heart still beating, it isn't worse – it isn't much better either. He has swapped one potential grave for another.

The truck engine turns over and revs. When the vehicle lurches forward onto the road, a couple of boxes topple on top of them, the sound dulled by the buffer of their bodies. Jan herds loose oranges with his feet in the dark, to stop them rolling. Nothing must alert the driver to his illicit cargo until they're over the Channel, the Sleeve, through Dover, in the UK.

While they were moving across Europe, he and Dlo, Jan kept alive an image of their destination, an imaginary hostel in Britain, in London or Birmingham. He emphasises the last syllable as he pronounces 'Birmingham' in his mind. London, London – everyone wants London, but someone from Jan's home village lives in Birmingham.

He didn't know the guy well back in Syria, but everyone knows his story – the visa, the language classes, the opportunities to earn money, the safety. Even if you break the law, you have rights. A lawyer will speak for you, there in Birmingham. And, needless to say, no bombs are falling, no gunfire rocks the night. There, modestly at first, Jan will begin. The room he pictures is not large or luxurious. He sees a bed, a table where he will prepare food and eat, and a desk where he will study to improve his English. OK, maybe the desk is asking too much. The desk can come later. In the early days, he will study at the table where he eats. He will move the plates to the sink and wash them immediately. Water will flow from the tap and his room will be spotless. The bed is covered, he doesn't know why, with a pink quilt. Where did it come from, this pink coverlet in his mind? He doesn't like it. Perhaps he once saw a photograph in a magazine and, at least for now, in his imagination, in the quiet room he dreams of, he is stuck with it. It was on the pink quilt that he rested his head at the end of each long day of their trek. It was for the cup, the English china cup, that he reached in his imagination, there where it stood on the table beside the pink bed in Birmingham.

Nothing is real in the freezer. The bed in Birmingham is not real, but neither are Jan's feet or his memories. Is he tired or is his brain freezing? Even in the heat of Hasakah, your blood could run cold, as the saying goes. Terror can do that to you. There's a crack, like the echo of long-ago gunfire in his mind. And then a flash. But it's not his memory. It's the door of the freezer truck. As it opens, Jan sees a policewoman, her back turned to them. She's so sure there's no one in this truck that she's not even looking as she pulls the door ajar. They blink in the mild night gleam. As she turns round, before she realises that they are there, Dlo leans into the opening gap, his face frozen into a clown's grin.

'*Bonjour!*' he bellows at her.

She screams and leaps back, many metres back, an unearthly spring in reverse. Her one colleague wrenches the door wide, another steadies the policewoman. She claps her hand over her mouth. She's laughing.

The men climb out of the orange truck onto empty road, shaking stiff limbs. The truck driver is yelling in French at one of the policemen, but he breaks off and storms over to their little group. He glares at each of them in turn and then spits at them. Jan makes as if to punch him, but Dlo holds him back and a policeman pulls the driver away. The policewoman, still laughing, socks Dlo on the arm.

'No Dover for you tonight,' she tells him. 'Better luck next time.'

Her colleague tells her to stop laughing and then turns to the refugees.

'You can die in here!' he shouts at them in English, striking the truck with his fist. 'Die!' He gestures at the driver. 'This guy will lock his truck and sleep five, six hours. Six hours in this cold? You will die!'

When they are loaded into the back of the police van, Jan pushes Dlo to the end of the bench and sits beside him.

'*Bonjour!*' says one of the others, and they all laugh. Dlo is the hero of the hour.

Jan laughs with them. 'You don't know this guy,' he tells the others. 'You don't know how funny he is, how smart.'

'*Bonjour!*' the guys repeat every now and then on the drive back to Calais, laughing every time. They can't see that Dlo, by Jan's side, is weeping.

III. FIRE IN THE SAND

This shabby truck will be stopped for sure. Jan has been on several like it. They're easy to open and easy to hide in, so the police and the border guards always stop them. But Jan must take every opportunity. His parents sold their property for him to get this far, their insurance for old age is gone, so he can't flag, he can't fear, he can't fail – he must push on. Plus, of course, he must stay on the safe side of the smuggler who drove him here and who wouldn't take kindly to his refusing. And after all, he reminds himself, Walat made it. Walat the Fearless. He's there now, in UK. He left the camp one night, scrambled into a truck by himself – because Walat had no money for smugglers – and got across. It's Walat who sleeps under the pink quilt on the bed Jan dreams of.

There's a boy this time, among the seven refugees planning to climb into this rattletrap truck. It's the boy's first attempt and his bravado is unconvincing.

'Listen,' Jan tells the boy softly in Kurdish, pointing. 'That driver, he's the one with the most to lose.'

The boy turns his big eyes up at Jan. He doesn't get it.

'We are refugees from Syria,' Jan reminds him. 'What can the police do to us? But him, that driver, he's the one committing a crime. Trafficking, people smuggling. He's the one who would go to prison.'

'And he's the one who makes the most money,' says another guy in the group. Another guy, not Dlo. For the first time, Jan will climb into a truck without Dlo. Every one of the long nights waiting for trucks by the side of dark roads, Jan had waited with Dlo. Every failed effort, Dlo and Jan. Together near Spain, together heading for Belgium, banging on the side of the truck before they could be driven over the wrong border into disaster. Now, today's truck – old, noisy, loose pieces rattling – Dlo could have breathed in this truck. Air comes in through the cracks. But instead he's breathing on the train back to Germany. The night of the freezer truck was too much for Dlo.

'I can't do this again, Jan. My terrible luck. Next time, I'll die for sure.'

'Where has your brain gone?' Jan asked him. 'Your number-one mind?'

Dlo looked away. 'I tell you, I can't do this, Jan.'

'Don't tell me about luck, Dlo. This is superstitious bullshit.'

'You can call it whatever you like.'

Should Jan have gone with his friend back to Germany? Dlo hadn't asked, but then Dlo never does ask. He has the brains while Jan has... What? The muscle, the courage and also, not to be forgotten, the English he learned from watching action movies long ago while Dlo studied.

How many more nights will he spend on the road, Jan asks himself, before he concedes defeat and heads back to Germany to join Dlo? One month? He's been saying 'One month, maximum!' since they arrived in Calais three months ago. Germany, though? His heart sinks. In UK, he figures it will take him six months to brush up his English and get a job. But in Germany, starting over, four years to learn the language? Five? He doesn't have the time. He must begin his interrupted life.

The truck brakes for the first roadblock. Jan puts his hand on the boy's shoulder. Through the gaps in the truck's sides, light seeps in from the police torches. But no one opens the door and the truck pulls off again, rumbling down the motorway.

Jan can see the whites of the boy's eyes as he stares. 'Can you speak English?' Jan asks him in English.

'Yes,' the boy says.

'That's good,' says Jan. 'Can you count?'

Jan has become an expert at stilling fear, after all these months of calming his friend Dlo. Jan can remember his own fear when he was quite a bit younger than this boy, maybe six or seven, living in the village, long before the family moved to the city, before he met Dlo. One of his tasks, after walking back from school, after taking the goats out to graze, was to load the empty pots onto the donkey cart to collect water from another village. He dreaded it. The stubborn donkey wouldn't walk on, wouldn't hurry, and night would be closing in while he pumped water into the pots. Always night, Jan thinks. Always darkness. The town square with Dlo eating cashews. The mortar blowing up the neighbours' house in the night in Hasakah. The boat from Turkey across the sea to Greece. All these nights waiting for trucks or waiting in trucks or running from trucks. Darkness! And then sleeping through the daylight to spend another night standing under dripping trees while the smuggler finds a truck. The boy on the cart gripped the reins of the donkey that plodded through the sudden strangeness where the dark had erased the familiar world. Far away, Jan, the boy Jan, used to see fires where people were burning oil in the sand. Now that many villages have emptied, desperate people are doing it again, drawing something from the sand to sell.

He's ready to climb down when they reach the second roadblock, but once more the police ignore their truck. Are they stupid, these police? Are they lazy? This truck might as well bear the slogan *Refugees on board*. And the third roadblock – nothing. Now they sense the incline as their cronky old truck – beloved truck! – drives up the ramp and onto the ferry. Feel that! Jan mimes with his hands the sway of the sea beneath them, explaining to the boy. But it may all come to nothing. How many refugees have been found in Dover and sent back to Calais? Too many to count. 'Be still,' the men in the truck tell each other. 'Not yet.'

As the truck drives out of Dover, Jan's UK SIM card connects and his mobile tells him that he has 3G. He texts his mother: *Today, I greet you from under UK sky.*

They wait until the truck pulls over for fuel, a full forty minutes, before they bang on the sides and the driver – too surprised to be angry – releases them. There's no sunshine as such, but it is daylight, not darkness. And it is UK.

Jan takes the boy with him. They set out on foot along the hard shoulder of the motorway, where it's too noisy to talk. Before long, a traffic cop pulls over next to them.

'What are you doing?' the cop yells against the roar of the passing traffic. 'You can't walk here.'

Jan stoops to peer into the vehicle.

'It's illegal,' the cop shouts at him.

Jan grins at him. 'I too am illegal,' he tells the cop in English. 'And this boy is illegal. Arrest us!'

He's in a police station somewhere, he has no idea where but in UK for sure, trying on some dry shoes from a kind policeman, when he sees a text on his mobile screen from Dlo.

Do you miss me yet? How is Calais?

Expect Me

Alghali steps into the dark room. Mr Dishman shuffles along behind him.

'Sit over there.'

Alghali sits where he has sat on each of his visits. From the worn-out rocking chair, which can't rock because Mr Dishman's old encyclopedia volumes are in the way, he can see a little bit of the small garden. The curtains are drawn but not fully open.

'Did you do the homework?'

Alghali takes the exercise book out of his bag and hands it over. Mr Dishman needs a while to make it to the other armchair. He sits and takes the book.

'Oh, my glasses.'

Alghali looks around, rises and picks them up from the dining-room table.

'Thanks.'

Mr Dishman's hands are shaking and the glasses won't stay on his nose, slipping off again and again. Alghali leans back and clasps his hands in his lap.

The old man's eyes study the lines in the book closely.

The exercises were set in his own neat handwriting, spidery and tidy, the gaps that needed filling in underlined.

'You asked someone?'

'No.'

'Internet?'

'Just the dictionary.'

Mr Dishman ticks off each line and hands the book back, pleased.

'Now tell me about your week.'

It is like this every time. Alghali has to talk about his life to practise his English. He has to do it in complete sentences, then Mr Dishman will review overall accomplishment and leave dated remarks in the exercise book. He is not a man fond of giving praise. Alghali has learned to take his time. It is not the telling; it is the accuracy of his expression Mr Dishman values. He is strict but he is not unreasonable, he helps along when necessary.

'Last week you said you were expecting a visitor?'

'Yes. My friend who is in Birmingham called me last week. He arranged to come and visit me here.'

'How long have you known each other?'

'I have known him for six months. We met when we first arrived in Italy. It was a coincidence.'

'How so?'

'He ran into me. I was standing with two friends at a street corner.'

'Did he have any news from your other friends?'

There is nothing new to add, but Alghali explains it again. Only two of their group have made it to England, he and Nabil, or Obama as he liked to call himself before they arrived. Here they are nameless; it doesn't matter what they call themselves, they disappear and dissolve. Here it is muteness. It doesn't have a name. Alghali wonders what Mr Dishman has made of his, whether he can say Alghali, or if he is just the Sudanese, the refugee. He only ever calls him 'young chap' or says, 'Well done, son.' It is clear that he is not Mr Dishman's son, which in itself is a good thing, for both of them.

The rest of Alghali's former group, the young men he travelled with through Europe, are still in Calais, attempting the journey across the Channel night after night.

Mr Dishman's hand reaches back up for the glasses and pulls them off with great effort.

'It is illegal. The way you are entering the country.'

He says it as if Alghali is responsible for everyone, as if he knows each person who's trying to get here. They have had this conversation before.

'There is no other way.'

It always ends the same; Alghali has nothing to add. Mr Dishman will talk about how Europe is being overrun and eventually he will pour Alghali a glass of water.

Alghali comes twice a week. Once with his English homework, the second time with his library books on accounting standards and UK policies. He wants to be ready for when the papers come through – they have to – for when he can resume his life. He was the top of his class and entered straight into a prestigious job. Financial manager. It was unheard of. He had impressed them all during the interview.

Mr Dishman makes him work through the accounting books paragraph by paragraph. With the dictionary he helps Alghali to understand the different laws in this country. But today it's grammar and conversational English. And since Alghali's exercises were flawless there is nothing else to do but talk.

'How are your flatmates?'

'They are all fine, thank you.'

Alghali wants to ask things but there is no time for this in their arrangement. Their schedule is usually packed tight, like the flat Mr Dishman lives in. There is another room, but Mr Dishman has taken to sleeping in the lounge. It's closer to the kitchen and bathroom. At ninety-four he is still agile but he is not young.

'They enjoyed the visit from my friend Nabil. He stayed overnight.'

Mr Dishman pushes the saucer with biscuits across the little table. He has insisted, since Alghali's first visit, that he should bring nothing but his classwork. As always, Alghali declines the biscuits. He does not want to be a bother.

'You are quiet today.'

'I'm sorry.'

Alghali takes the exercise book and hands it over.

'What is next week's homework? Perhaps I don't stay too long today.'

'Why not?'

'I don't want to disturb you.'

When they talk about their week, it is apparent how similar the surfaces of their lives have become. Nothing happens other than in the past. Or in the future, for Alghali. The distant future that could come tomorrow, that could come months down the line.

Or never.

The emptiness waiting produces is best filled with structure and discipline. This is Mr Dishman's belief. Alghali does not disagree.

At the weekend, Nabil teased him about his time with the pensioner. The old man wasn't the problem, but his attitude.

'Why put yourself through it?'

'I want to learn.'

'From him?'

'From who else?'

Alghali thinks about the present that stretches as endlessly as the plains at home. Although at home it is pleasant, broken by mountains and hills, by village life, by living in the bustling city, by family.

Here the present stretches over trips to the library, free online courses to keep the mind engaged. Mr Dishman's strictness is somewhat absurd, but it is an exchange. However little, something is kept alive.

'You cannot disturb me when we have agreed for you to come.'

Alghali doesn't respond. Mr Dishman tries again.

'What else happened?'

'I went to the library.'

'Today or yesterday?'

They aren't always this fragmented, Alghali's answers. He often takes his time, but only to think about syntax and grammar. He comes prepared with things to talk about, anecdotes from his flatmates, other Sudanese men he hadn't known before his arrival in Bolton.

Alghali often tells Mr Dishman about Bolton, the streets he is discovering. Mr Dishman was born and raised here, but it is different, seeing your city through a stranger's eyes. Sometimes Mr Dishman allows questions about his own life, after a successful class, and their conversation takes a different turn. On those rare occasions they acknowledge silently how confined their lives are. The few things that break the routine of nothingness. For Mr Dishman there is bridge, always on a Wednesday, always at Mrs Gray's house. There are the carers, the food deliveries for the heavier groceries, the odd stroll to the park. Alghali attends English lessons, his *real* English lessons, also twice a week but shorter; there are his walks, talking with his flatmates and friends, and the occasional trip to the lawyer to enquire about his pending case.

It was at one of his English lessons that they met. The teacher had distributed leaflets in the neighbourhood calling for people willing to help with conversational English classes.

It has been months, the same routine. Never in Alghali's life has he been this static.

They don't call it visits, although most of the time is spent talking about the now of Alghali's life. Admittedly, his life is still more active than Mr Dishman's. It does have friendships and laughter. It does have a connection to the future, whether here or not.

'Are you unwell?' Mr Dishman asks.

Alghali looks at him. Mr Dishman has asked for details of his real life, the one underneath, the details that belong to the journey here, to the before. But Mr Dishman is never quite ready to really hear them.

'I found out that a young friend died.'

'Back home? In Sudan?'

'No, in Calais. He was trying to make it over here.'

Mr Dishman's hands smooth over his wispy hair.

'A glass of water?'

Alghali nods. 'I'll get it?'

Mr Dishman agrees. Alghali goes into the kitchen, which has not been changed since the house was built. It is small but everything is to hand, laid out by the carers who come to support Mr Dishman twice a day. He returns with both their glasses.

'How old was he?'

'Fourteen.'

Why he has come today he doesn't know. They have each other's numbers, so they can call if anything in their arrangement needs changing. They have never done so. It was the wrong day to break the habit that has become what holds them both in place these days.

'He said he was nineteen when I met him but I knew it couldn't be true. Still, I didn't know he was that young. He was about to come here, lawfully. To be with his brother.'

Mr Dishman is quiet and puts the glass back on the side table. His eyes follow a squirrel in the garden.

'Perhaps you could open the curtains for me after all.'

Alghali walks to the doors that open into the garden. The light changes the room; it immediately feels more spacious.

'The law is changing. He would have been able to enter the country once his papers were confirmed.' He sits back down. 'Five months in the Jungle. Adnan couldn't wait any longer, he climbed on top of a train.'

Mr Dishman's reply is sudden, quicker than usual. 'That boy? It was in the papers yesterday, a young man was electrocuted.'

'Yes.' Alghali puts his exercise book in his bag and rises. 'It is the same boy.'

He thinks about the teenager's nervous confidence. He had wondered why he was travelling by himself, at his age, without family. It wouldn't have surprised him to learn he wanted to pioneer the journey for the rest of his family.

'Would you excuse me, please?'

Mr Dishman walks Alghali to the door, a hand on his shoulder.

'I'm very sorry.'

At the open door they hurry to get away, to leave the awkward moment between them: Alghali towards the street, Mr Dishman back inside the flat.

'Thursday, as usual?'

'I will see you then, thank you.'

The sun has no strength at this time of the year but it is still pleasing. The colours return after the muted lounge. Alghali shoulders his bag and walks in the opposite direction to his flat, which is at the other end of the road. He takes the short cut under the bridge and enters the park. A pool of rainwater that has collected in an unused fountain by his favourite bench reflects the setting sun. There are a few people scattered around, mostly dog owners taking their pets for an evening stroll. A couple of young men walk along the path. They look tired but happy to leave the working week behind.

'*As-salaam 'alaykum*.' Alghali picks up after the first ring. 'I have heard. From Nabil.'

They are silent, on both ends of the phone. Suleyman, his friend, is still in Calais. For five months there has been no luck, no making it through. Alghali thinks of Mr Dishman. He would be content about the lack of success of what he calls illegal activity. Yet he would be equally firm and reliable with Suleyman should he come and desire to learn the language, 'but properly'.

Alghali gets up again and walks to the other exit, which leads out on to a small residential street. There are no people there until he gets to a little roundabout with an off-licence and a launderette.

'Nabil found his brother. The number you gave him was right.'

The next street is a little bigger, with a pub at the next corner. The street lights have come on and with it the Friday evening activities have started.

Nabil told Alghali that Adnan had travelled with his whole family – five of them. The parents and three siblings. All drowned off the coast of Lampedusa; only the teenager made it ashore. They had teased him, Nabil, Suleyman and the others, because Adnan had always talked about his older brother in England. The strange obsession had annoyed them at times. 'My brother this', 'my brother that'.

'We will visit Adnan's brother, Nabil and I,' Alghali says.

It is completely dark now. Alghali promises to call again later.

He enjoys it most when he gets lost in the maze of residential streets, when he forgets how he got here, where he is supposed to go next. This type of nothingness is one of discovery, not impotence.

There is a bottle of water in his bag and an apple. He sits next to a woman watching a group of teenage girls.

'They shouldn't be out this late. Especially now.'

He agrees. It is dark. People are getting drunk. It is Friday, at the end of a long week.

'I better be off myself.' She disappears into the alley a few houses further down.

Alghali moves on as well. Back in his neighbourhood the supermarket is still busy and the two betting shops are just closing. The men from the park earlier are standing by the local pub but they are not drinking. Alghali half nods. There is no response. They look as if they haven't seen him. His phone rings again. Nabil is calling more often than usual. Adnan was like his little brother. It isn't easy for any of them, but Nabil will take it the hardest.

'*As-salaam 'alaykum.*'

A couple comes out of the pub to smoke. The man shields the flame, the woman bends and twists for the cigarette to catch.

Alghali stops and listens to Nabil's rapid words.

'I'll call you tomorrow. Don't worry, we will make it there, *inshallah*. Try and sleep.'

He moves on and passes the pub. One of the young men walks into him. Alghali has not yet returned the phone to his jacket pocket and he finds himself face to face with this unfamiliar person. It is close, he can see the details of the man's face, the clear eyes, the supple skin. The breath smells of chewing gum. Mint.

'What do you have to say for yourself?'

Alghali stumbles, surprised. 'I don't understand.'

The couple have finished their cigarette and return to the bar inside.

'What have your people done this time?'

The other two are closing in on his back. The one speaking comes even closer. Alghali shields his genitals in reflex. It is quick and sudden, without any flourish.

The one in front punches him in the stomach.

'For Paris.'

They stroll away as quiet as before in the park. Alghali coughs, his knees give way and he hits the paving. There is no noise outside except for the occasional wisp of music, the occasional laughter or drunken cheer from the pub. The thin legs enter his view first; they stop, towering over his face. Alghali's hands are flat on the ground, helping him to steady his breath.

'It is too late for you to be walking in this neighbourhood.'

Mr Dishman leans his stick against the wall and extends a hand. Alghali shakes his head and pulls himself up.

'Nothing happened.'

He doesn't want another lecture. He doesn't need to hear more about the dangers of Islam to British society. Or Mr Dishman's forceful opinions. How people are rightfully scared, and how some, inevitably, will take matters into their own hands. Not tonight.

'I was on my way to you.'

'Why?'

'You haven't heard?'

They are now standing by Alghali's door. He is unsure what to do. The old man has never come up here; they always meet at Mr Dishman's house, at arranged times.

'A terrorist attack in Paris.'

'When?'

'An hour ago. It seems a man coming through the refugee route was involved.'

He still doesn't understand. Why is Mr Dishman here? What does he want? He is right, after all, now he has proof. He has always told him, 'You can't trust everyone. Not all are decent men like you, young chap. Many that are on their way don't have good intentions.'

'That's very bad news. Thanks for letting me know. I will watch the news later. You should go back home. It's cold.'

'It was a Syrian man.'

Alghali looks at him. Mr Dishman's unsteadiness has given way to determination.

'I'm not from Syria.'

'People don't make that distinction.' Mr Dishman's milky eyes look right at him. He is repeating what Alghali has told him. How he is mistaken, when need be, for anyone, to fit a description. 'Be careful.' He fetches his stick. 'I will see you on Thursday?'

The old man is already moving towards the other end of the street. He is slow and deliberate.

'Yes, Thursday, thank you.'

*

It is dark in his room. He lies on the bed without switching the light on, his eyes seeking out the ceiling. After a while he can make out the contours of the narrow wardrobe on the other side.

Everything has changed.

Suleyman is waiting for his call but Alghali doesn't have the words to talk. He sends another text.

Our lives are this now. Never really home.

Suleyman's reply comes in an instant.

Expect me. One way or another.

Acknowledgements

Many people helped to create this slim book. Warm thanks to those we can't name, as well as to:

Tanya Abramsky, Mary Beattie and Elke, Tara Beattie, Julian Borger, Stephanie Brooks, Carolyn Dempster, Irene Garrow (English PEN), Emma Graham-Harrison, Sheila Hayman (Write to Life), Mazeda Hossain, Zimako Jones, Gabrielle Le Roux, Shaun Levin, Pontso Mafethe, Wakil Omar, Helen Simpson, Terence McGinity, Corinne Squire and – for everything from concept to completion – our publisher and editor, Meike Ziervogel.

Peirene

Contemporary European Literature. Thought provoking, well designed, short.

'Two-hour books to be devoured in a single sitting: literary cinema for those fatigued by film.' TLS

Online Bookshop

Subscriptions

Literary Salons

Reading Guides

Publisher's Blog

www.peirenepress.com

Follow us on twitter and Facebook @PeirenePress
Peirene Press is building a community of passionate readers.
We love to hear your comments and ideas.
Please email the publisher at: meike.ziervogel@peirenepress.com

Subscribe

Peirene Press publishes series of world-class contemporary novellas. An annual subscription consists of three books chosen from across the world connected by a single theme.

The books will be sent out in December (in time for Christmas), May and September. Any title in the series already in print when you order will be posted immediately.

The perfect way for book lovers to collect all the Peirene titles.

'A class act.' GUARDIAN

'Two-hour books to be devoured in a single sitting: literary cinema for those fatigued by film.' TLS

£35   1 Year Subscription (3 books, free p&p)

£65   2 Year Subscription (6 books, free p&p)

£90   3 Year Subscription (9 books, free p&p)

Peirene Press, 17 Cheverton Road, London N19 3BB
T 020 7686 1941
E subscriptions@peirenepress.com

www.peirenepress.com/shop
with secure online ordering facility

COUNTERPOINTS ARTS

Peirene Press is proud to support
Counterpoints Arts.

Counterpoints Arts is a charity that promotes the
creative arts by and about refugees and migrants
in the UK.

---

*'We are living in a time of human
displacement. We need bold and
imaginative interventions to help
us make sense of migration. And
who better to do this than artists
who are engaging with this issue.'*

ALMIR KOLDZIC AND ÁINE O'BRIEN, DIRECTORS, COUNTERPOINTS ARTS

By buying this book you are helping
Counterpoints Arts enhance the cultural
integration of refugees – a mission which will
surely change our society for the better.

Peirene will donate 50p from the sale of this
book to the charity.

www.counterpointsarts.org.uk